LONE RIDER

OTHER FIVE STAR WESTERN TITLES BY LEWIS B. PATTEN:

LONE RIDER

A WESTERN DUO

LEWIS B. PATTEN

FIVE STAR

A part of Gale, Cengage Learning

GALE
CENGAGE Learning·

Farmington Hills, Mich • San Francisco • New York • Waterville, Maine
Meriden, Conn • Mason, Ohio • Chicago

GALE
CENGAGE Learning·

LIBRARY OF CONGRESS CATALOGING-IN-PUBLICATION DATA

Patten, Lewis B.
  [Novels. Selections]
  Lone rider : a western duo / Lewis B. Patten. — First edition.
    pages ; cm
    ISBN 978-1-4328-2846-2 (hardcover) — ISBN 1-4328-2846-0 (hardcover)
    I. Title.
PS3566.A79A6 2015
813'.54—dc23   2015008074

First Edition. First Printing: July 2015.
Published in conjunction with Golden West Literary Agency.
Find us on Facebook– https://www.facebook.com/FiveStarCengage
Visit our website– http://www.gale.cengage.com/fivestar/
Contact Five Star™ Publishing at FiveStar@cengage.com

Printed in the United States of America
1 2 3 4 5 6 7 19 18 17 16 15

CONTENTS

★ ★ ★ ★ ★

WHERE THE BACKSHOOTER WAITS

★ ★ ★ ★ ★

I

Stuart Dawson reined in at the head of the street and stared at the drowsy, sleepy town with somber eyes, asking himself sourly: *Where did I fail, and how?* He hated the task before him today as he had hated none of the similar tasks that had gone before. Because at last, today, he had faced facts in his mind, had come to the realization that there must be an end to this—and soon.

Castle Rock snuggled on a flat place beside Snake River, the bluff from which it got its name sheltering it on the north. Main Street was wide and dusty, lined with business establishments here at the upper end, with saloons and other places of amusement down at the lower end. The bank occupied one corner of Fourth and Main, directly across from the Stockman's Hotel.

Stuart's wide shoulders lifted in a shrug, and he made a light grimace of distaste as he nudged his horse into movement. The sun beat against his wide shoulders, and the heat of the day had dampened his khaki shirt until it showed dark across his back and chest and beneath his arms. He wore dusty Levi's and boots, and a shapeless, wide-brimmed black hat.

He dismounted first before the Palace, tied his horse, and shouldered impatiently through the doors. He put his harsh glance on Dutch Stranski and asked shortly: "Well, how much is it this time?"

"Seven hundred. A little more'n that, but we'll call it square for seven hundred." Dutch was bald, and he needed a shave. There was a cynical coarseness about his features that Stuart found repellent. He said: "All right. I'll square it this one time. But it's the last. If you let Matt play in here on tick any more, I'll take it out of your hide."

Dutch's eyes said: *Anytime. Just anytime.* But his mouth made a rueful grin and his lips formed the words: "Sure, Stu. Anything you say. Have a drink on the house. The beer's cold."

Stuart gave him a level look that made no effort to conceal his dislike. He said, turning: "I'll pay for mine. And I'll drink them somewhere else."

He went out into the street, angry, but feeling helpless, too. He paused long enough to make a cigarette and light it. Then he headed back upstreet afoot toward the bank. He went through the wide door, touched his hat to a woman customer waiting at the barred cashier's window, and then strode toward Iles's office in the rear.

Hang Matt anyway. He knew as well as anyone that Anvil didn't have money in the bank to draw on. He knew, but he didn't care. As long as Stuart was willing to square his gambling debts for him, he didn't care.

Stuart pushed into Jack Iles's office, thumbed his hat back off his sweating forehead, and sank down into the oak chair across the desk from the portly banker.

Iles was a short man. His genial smile did not quite extend to his eyes, which were the blue of ice floes in the river in March. His two front teeth were large, and showed as he smiled at Stuart. He said: "How much is it this time, Stu?"

"Seven hundred," Stuart murmured wearily. "But this is going to be the last. It can't go on. I'll be hanged if I'll let him push the year's profits over Stranski's gambling tables without putting up a scrap."

Iles gave him a long, questioning stare. His voice showed mild amazement. "You mean it this time, don't you?"

"You're blamed right I mean it." Stuart tossed his cigarette into the brass spittoon beside the desk and began to make another. His hands, he noticed, were trembling, so he dropped them below the level of the desk while he finished making the cigarette. He said: "Give me another thousand, and make a note for it. I'll settle up at shipping time."

"Sixty days, then?"

Stuart nodded absently. Iles got up and went into the vault at the rear of the bank. When he returned, he carried a sheaf of banknotes in one hand, a blank note in the other. He sat down and wrote rapidly on the note in his neat, small handwriting. He pushed the note toward Stuart, and Stuart scrawled his signature.

He realized that he still held the cigarette in his hand, unlit. He wiped a match alight on his jeans and held it to the cigarette. Iles shoved the money across the table at him. Stuart counted it, then tucked it down into his shirt pocket.

Iles stood up. "Stu, I hope you mean that about Matt. Because I've gone in about as heavy as I want to. You know Anvil owes almost everybody in town, besides the eleven thousand it owes the bank. You can pay it off and have money to spare in the fall if prices stay up. If they take a drop, you'll be in trouble."

"I know, Jack. I know." Stuart didn't take Iles's lecture too seriously because he got one every time he came into the bank. But he did take seriously Matt and Matt's gambling. Because with Matt it wasn't even gambling. Matt never won. He invariably lost, and the profits from Anvil, from Stuart's hard work, from the hard work of the whole crew, went to pay his losses. It had to stop. There were other uses for Anvil's profits. . . .

Stuart went out of the bank and turned again toward the Palace. But this time, when he entered, he saw Matt, his brother, facing Stranski across the bar, one of his hands flat upon it. He heard Matt's voice: "You heard me, Dutch. Double or nothing.

11

What'll it be?"

Stranski said—"Heads."—and Matt lifted his hand. Stuart could see the way his face fell, and knew he had lost.

Stuart walked to the bar, frowning, and fished the thick packet of banknotes from his shirt. He counted out $700 on the bar and shoved it toward Dutch. "Here it is, but this is the last. If Matt wants to play from here on, be sure you see the color of his money before you let him."

Stranski made no move toward the money. He was grinning, showing his yellowed, gold-capped front teeth. He said: "It's fourteen hundred now, Stu. Didn't you just see me win that double or nothing toss from Matt?"

Stuart picked up the seven hundred and returned it to his pocket. He growled—"I warned you."—and turned on his heel.

Matt spun him around, and Matt's young, handsome face was contorted with rage. Matt's temper let loose and his fist smashed into Stuart's mouth. Stuart staggered back, and sprawled on the sawdust floor. He got up, and calmly wiped the blood from his lips with the back of his hand. He said: "There's a job on Anvil for you, Matt, but there'll be no more hand-outs."

He stared at his younger brother, wondering again where he had failed, where he had taken the wrong turning. Matt glowered at him, a little taller than Stuart, and handsomer with his dark, curly hair, his reckless, laughing eyes. But his eyes weren't laughing now. They were sullen and filled with resentful anger. And they showed briefly another emotion, one entirely ugly under the circumstances. Hatred.

That was like a blow to Stuart. It shocked him to see that in Matt's eyes. He turned abruptly and strode from the saloon.

Outside, it seemed he couldn't get away quickly enough. He mounted and swung his horse northward and galloped out of town. There was heaviness in his heart, heaviness and hopelessness and wonder.

He put the town behind him, left the road, and let his horse pick its way through the ocean of gray-green sagebrush. The sun went under a bank of cloud, and the air cooled perceptibly afterward. But Stuart rode, head down, unnoticing. His mind kept going back—going back to the beginning in an effort to solve that look of naked hatred in Matt's young eyes.

II

The story of their father had been the story of a dozen men in the early mining camps of Colorado. Except that Lucky Dawson—he wasn't called Lucky then—brought along his wife and two small sons when he came West in the early 1870s. He settled in Denver, in a tiny log cabin in the Cherry Creek bottoms near where the creek flows into the Platte. And leaving his wife and sons, struck out for Leadville, alone.

There followed nearly two years of privation for the lone woman and her two small sons. Lucky sent them no money. He had none to send. He worked in the mines at Leadville for a bare $5 a day, and the high cost of food in the mining camp ate up all of that. Stuart's mother took in washing, took cleaning jobs in Denver Hotels, took anything, indeed, that would keep the bean pot boiling.

They heard from Lucky at intervals. He had staked a claim, and had quit his job to work it. He was back working in the mines for a day wage. He had quit again and was working his claim. It came as a complete surprise when, one night unannounced, he burst into the cabin door, both fists filled with goldback bills, his pockets and saddlebags filled with more— filled to overflowing. It seemed he had struck an unbelievably rich vein of lead, and had sold out to a syndicate for $70,090.

After that they moved. They moved into a three-storied Victorian mansion on F Street, a place with a grassy yard, a

13

wrought-iron fence, and two couchant lions to guard the door. Matt and Stu used to ride the lions, pretending they were horses, and the granite animals bore the marks of boys' heels on their ribs till the day they were carted away and junked.

There followed a period of extreme prosperity. Everything Lucky Dawson touched seemed to turn to gold. He bought and sold mining claims from South Park to Vasquez. Matt, being the younger of the two boys, naturally received the bulk of his mother's attention. She dressed him in black velvet suits and patent leather shoes. She lavished upon him a lifetime's frustrated desire for fine clothes, since she was by now too old and too thickened by age to wear clothes gracefully herself. Also, she was never accepted into Denver society. Too many people remembered her from her washing and cleaning days. And so naturally the kids in the neighborhood made life tough for young Matt. At least twice a week he would come home with his nose bloodied and his clothing in tatters.

There is a limit to how many beatings the human spirit can stand. With Matt it was never a case of fighting but one boy. There were always three or four. Until Stuart took a hand. In that was perhaps born Matt's resentment of his older brother, his feeling of inferiority to Stuart. For Stuart did what Matt alone had never been able to do. He instilled respect in the neighborhood kids and they began to let Matt alone.

There was Mercy Jones, who, at eleven, Matt thought he could not live without. Stuart captured her heart without even trying. And then the Ute tribes were moved out of Colorado and onto a barren reservation in eastern Utah, and their Colorado lands opened for settlement. Lucky Dawson was one of the many who came to stake homesteads on the new land. He was one of the few who had more in his pockets than his empty hands.

He staked on Toadstool Creek, sent clear to Texas for a herd of cattle, clear to Missouri for a dozen Hereford bulls. And as the years passed, he bought up the lands of his less fortunate neighbors. So that when he died, he was one of the richest men in western Colorado. His Anvil brand sprawled across the lean hips of ten thousand cattle.

Dying, with Stuart and Matt at his bedside, he whispered hoarsely to Stuart: "Look out for Matt. He's like his ma, and there ain't much strength to him." It was a fallacy, built by the years of Matt's being babied by his mother, now in her grave almost five years. But Lucky Dawson said the words, and Matt heard them and believed.

When Matt was eighteen, he got into a scrape with a town girl to whom scrapes were no novelty. Stuart got him out of it. A year later, Matt got into a fight in a saloon in Castle Rock, and his opponent fell and hit his head on the bar rail, and died. Stuart got him out of that. Now, Stuart pondered the past, realizing for the first time that if blame must be laid somewhere, it must be laid, not at Matt's door, but at Stuart's and Lucky's and, too, at their dead mother's.

His mouth tasted bitter, and his head ached. Hard on Matt, this cutting off of support now. Matt was used to support in all things from Stuart. He had never learned to stand on his own two feet; he had not learned in his teens as he should. Learning now would be harder. Maybe too hard. $700 on the toss of a coin. Next time it might be $7,000. Matt had to learn to stand by himself before he bankrupted Anvil. Hating himself, Stuart rode into the home place.

Stuart was not so tall as Matt, and his hair was perhaps a few shades lighter. There was a certain solidity about Stuart that was very noticeable. His jaw was straight and hard, his body compact and solid. Even the level way his gray eyes studied you had its own peculiar quality of solidity. Solid and steady. The kind of man it took to assume the reins of a cattle empire with

15

never a break in the empire's stride. The kind of man who could make whatever he guided grow. Hard? Perhaps he was. No man succeeded in the West without a certain hardness in his make-up.

Norah Dawson, his wife, thought him too soft. Too soft where Matt was concerned. She resented that softness, his free generosity in paying Matt out of his scrapes. She resented it because Matt left nothing for the things Norah wanted, a new black buggy, the winters in the luxury of a Denver hotel. Trips to Europe, or New York.

A horse was tied before the house, a horse bearing the Q Bar brand of the town's livery stable. Stuart frowned a little as he climbed the porch steps.

He flung open the door. Roark Blankenship stepped away from Norah, flustered, and said quickly: "Oh, Stu. I've been waiting to see you."

"Looks like Norah's been making your wait pleasant," said Stuart drily.

"Stu, that's unfair." Yet Norah's voice lacked the proper amount of indignation.

"Is it?" He looked away from her pink face, her smoldering eyes. He put his glance on tall, darkly handsome Roark. Roark was a lawyer, Castle Rock's only lawyer in fact. He was a frequent visitor at Anvil since his services were frequently required to get Matt out of some scrape or other.

Stuart asked: "What was it you wanted to see me about, Roark?"

Roark shrugged, still not fully at ease but rapidly becoming so. "Matt. What else?"

"What is it this time?"

"The company he keeps. If you don't know it, you ought to."

Stuart grinned wearily. He said softly: "Get out of here, Roark. I know who Matt runs with and you know I know. That's a pretty thin excuse for being out here at Anvil. Fact is, you didn't expect me back for a while, did you?"

Norah stamped a small foot and started to speak, but Stuart cut her off with his curt: "Shut up. I didn't speak to you."

Roark said uneasily: "You're making too much of this, Stu."

"Am I?"

"Of course you are. There's nothing between Norah and me."

"Then stay away from Anvil. Stay away unless you're sent for."

Roark Blankenship flushed darkly. His glance touched Norah briefly, and there seemed to be some silent promise passing between them. Roark got his hat from the table and strode angrily toward the door. Clouds were gathering in Norah's beautiful face. Roark went out, and Stuart, standing utterly still, heard the pound of his horse's hoofs as he rode away.

Norah said: "Stu, how could you? I've never been so humiliated!"

"You were kissing him."

"What if I was?" Defiance made her tone sharp.

Stuart stared at her. She was a tall woman, coming to Stuart's chin when she stood close to him, which wasn't often these days. Her hair was as black as a Spaniard's, and her skin had an olive tint to it that made it very striking. Her eyes were dark, large, and soft usually. Tonight they were narrowed and hard. Her perfectly formed breasts rose and fell with her breathing, hastened by anger. She stormed: "I don't see how you can blame me for that. Marriage to you has been nothing but disappointment. I thought when I married you that Anvil. . . ."

Stuart interrupted: "You thought that Anvil would provide all the luxuries you'd never had before?"

"Well, yes, if you put it that way. But Matt pushes it all across the gambling tables at the Palace. There's never anything left for me."

17

"And infidelity is a solution?"

She slapped him, but her eyes could not quite meet his. She was angry, but her anger was tempered by guilt. Stuart felt a hollowness in the pit of his stomach. "It's gone farther than I thought, then?"

"Roark has promised me. . . ."

"Promised you what?"

She sat down on the leather-covered sofa. "Nothing."

Stuart yanked her to her feet. Suddenly he was very angry. "What has he promised you? The damn' fool hasn't got money enough to buy himself a new suit. What the devil do you think he can give you?"

She was smiling, silent. Her eyes mocked him. And he knew she had already said more than she intended, knew she would say no more.

He said: "There'll be no more hand-outs for Matt. In the fall when we ship, you can have your trip to New York and your new buggy. Maybe I've been unfair, Norah. I'll try to change."

Her smile didn't falter. "It's too late for that, Stu. It's too late."

He put his arms around her. She was pliant, but resisting, too. She was cold, and she turned her face from his kiss. He had the feeling that she was laughing at him.

He flung her away. He stalked outside, slamming the door behind. He mounted his horse and pounded furiously away from the house, out into the sea of gray-green sagebrush. And he had the oddest feeling, a new feeling. Almost like fear. With Matt hating, and Norah mocking, he knew he was utterly alone. And he knew self-blame because this was so.

Stuart rode north for a while, absently noting the condition of each Anvil cow or steer that he passed. Eventually, riding, his agitation vanished along with some of his depression. He had always been able to find solace for his troubles in riding this vast and empty land. For as far as the eye could see lay nothing but Anvil range, stocked with Anvil cattle and horses. On the slopes were thickets of scrub oak and sarvus, but here in the bottoms there was nothing but sage and greasewood.

Yet an odd uneasiness persisted in Stuart's consciousness. He tried to rationalize that and almost succeeded. He was worried about Matt, and depressed about Norah's infidelity, if it had gone that far. And these two things must be causing the peculiar feeling of unease.

Sundown came, and the sun gleamed, briefly gold, just above the horizon where there were no clouds. Then it sank from sight, and quickly the gray of dusk came down. Stuart turned his horse and headed back toward home.

The shot sounded almost immediately after that. It came from a thick clump of greasewood just before him. He saw the puff of smoke but he did not hear the shot. Something struck him in the head, and he toppled from his saddle. He did not even feel the impact as he hit the ground.

III

It was full dark when he awoke. He lay utterly still for a moment, wondering where he was. And then slowly it began to come back. He remembered the puff of smoke from that clump of greasewood. He remembered the staggering blow on his head.

A hand went to his head, and came away sticky and wet. He struggled to a sitting position, blinked as the world reeled before his eyes. His head felt as though a thousand hammers beat at his skull from the inside.

Slowly, gradually the reeling, moonlit world steadied. And Stuart's eye caught a gleam of something on the ground. Stolidly his hand went out and picked it up. A watch. A gold watch. He knew what inscription would be on the back even before he looked. *To Matt on his 18th birthday from Dad.* The chain was broken. The chain must have caught on that extended dead arm of brush there as Matt bent over him.

With his face cold, Stuart stuffed the watch into his pocket. Absently, automatically his hand went to his shirt pocket where the money had been. He smiled bitterly. He hadn't needed to feel for the money. He had known it would be gone. So Matt had gone this far. He had come to the point where he could kill his own brother for $1,000.

Stuart shook his savagely pounding head and stood up. He peered about him owlishly, and finally discovered his horse, grazing unconcernedly a hundred feet away. That grazing bullet had taken more of his strength than he had at first realized. He was exhausted by the time he reached the horse. He clung to the saddle horn for a full five minutes before he felt strong enough to mount. Automatically he turned the animal toward Anvil. His mind kept repeating: *I've got to think! I've got to think! What am I going to do?*

The answer was simple enough. Go to Castle Rock and prefer charges against Matt for attempted murder. Yet Stuart knew he'd never do that. He knew he wouldn't because Lucky had said as he died: "Look after Matt. . . ." And Stuart knew he wouldn't for another reason, too. Because he felt responsible himself for whatever Matt had become.

He headed toward Anvil, but passed the lamplit buildings without stopping. Dizziness kept him swaying in his saddle.

At the edge of town he left the road and angled over toward Toadstool Creek. At its edge he dismounted and kneeled down. He slopped cold water onto his face, onto the nasty, blood-caked bullet crease. It stung and throbbed.

Stuart stood up and dried his face and the side of his head with a clean bandanna. Then again he mounted and rode into Castle Rock, occasionally blotting the blood with the damp bandanna.

He guessed, pulling into Main Street, that he wanted to see Matt, to talk to him before he did anything else. He racked his horse before the Palace Saloon, and shouldered through the batwing doors.

Save for a drunken, sleeping oldster at one of the tables, the place was deserted. Stranski was mopping the bar, preparatory to closing up. His dealers and house men were gone and his gambling tables were covered with green cloths.

Stuart stood, swaying slightly, just inside the door. "Where's Matt?"

Dutch Stranski showed him a face that was regretful and sympathetic. "You ain't heard, Stu?"

"Heard what?"

Stranski coughed, and looked away. "I hate to be the one to tell you. . . ."

Stuart's spine felt cold. "Tell me what?"

"Why Matt's in jail, Stu."

"What for?"

"Murder. He killed Sam Brobaker and robbed his safe. Stu, you ought to've paid off for Matt this afternoon. He got to drinking and the more he drank the meaner he got. He kept cussing you, and finally he left."

"What time was that?"

"I'd say a little after five."

"You see him after that?"

Stranski seemed to hesitate. "I hate to do this, Stu. Seems like I'm putting a rope around Matt's neck. But I did see him again."

"When?"

"He came back in around eight-thirty. He seemed upset. I figured he'd just seen you. He paid me a thousand dollars on what he owed me."

Stuart felt suddenly empty, dead. "Then what?"

21

"He had a few more drinks, but he'd stopped cussing you. He went out again, and about ten-thirty, came back and paid me the other four hundred. He had more'n that, though. I'd guess he had close to a thousand that second time, too. I figured he'd got that from you, too. But he hadn't been here over twenty minutes when the sheriff came in and arrested him. Seems like Roark Blankenship seen him leaving Brobaker's and went in to talk to Sam and found him dead."

Stuart couldn't look at Stranski just then. He felt ashamed, and somehow guilty himself. He turned, wordless, and strode out into the night.

He should have noticed the difference in the town when he rode in. He noticed it now. Ordinarily at midnight, Castle Rock was dark and sleeping, except for the Palace and a couple of other smaller saloons. But tonight, there were lights in at least half the houses. On the hotel verandah, perhaps a dozen men were gathered, talking.

A block off Main, there were lights gleaming from the jail windows. And the men on the hotel verandah stopped talking and stared at Stuart as he passed, heading for the jail on foot.

There was a crowd around the jail, too, a crowd of almost twenty men. A few of them spoke grudgingly to Stuart. The jail door was locked. Stuart pounded on it with his fist.

He heard the sheriff's voice, muffled by the thickness of the door. "Who is it, and what do you want?"

"It's Stuart Dawson. Open up!"

Behind him he heard a man mutter sourly: "By hell, he won't be paying Matt out of this mess."

The door opened and the sheriff peered out. Immediately the door swung wide and Stuart went in. Sheriff Luke Bascomb slammed it quickly and shot the bolt. He put his back to the door and faced Stuart. He said the same words Stuart had heard outside: "You can't buy him out of this one, Stu."

Bascomb was a tall, gangling man, maybe forty-five. His eyes were a hard, blue-gray. Tonight he needed a shave, and gray showed in his whiskers prominently. He had a large, straight nose, a wide, thin-lipped mouth. His eyebrows were bushy, and they were graying, too. His hair was almost white. And Bascomb was scared. He said: "Folks in Castle Rock have stood all they're going to stand from Matt Dawson. I just hope they don't try to take him out of jail."

Stuart felt a raging anger. "Luke, if you let that happen, there's nothing in this world will save you from me."

He crossed the room to the cell-block at the rear. Matt Dawson looked up from the bench where he sat. At sight of Stuart, his face took on a resentful look that changed almost immediately to one of bewilderment. He said: "I knew you'd come."

Stuart frowned. Matt had showed no surprise at seeing him alive. He had showed no guilt, and no fear. His chief emotion seemed to have been relief. Stuart fished the watch from his pocket. "I believe this is yours."

Matt got up, crossed the cell to the barred door, and took the proffered watch. He began to wind it absently and, when he had finished, asked: "What time you got?"

Stuart told him and Matt set the watch. He started to stuff it into his pocket and then noticed the broken chain. Stuart was looking at the belt loop on Matt's Levi's for the other half, but it wasn't there.

Matt asked: "Where the devil did you get this? From Stranski?"

Stuart grinned noncommittally.

Matt said: "You paid him off, then?"

"He says you did. And I didn't get the watch from him. Someone took a shot at me tonight, robbed me of a thousand dollars, and dropped the watch beside me as they got the money

23

out of my pocket." He turned his head so that Matt could see the angry, red bullet burn.

Matt scowled. "You think I did that?" His expression told Stuart that he was increasingly puzzled.

Stu meant to say: *Did you?* But he didn't say it. Instead, the words came out: "No. I did think so, but I don't any more. I want to ask you something else. Did you pay Stranski anything on that gambling debt tonight?"

"How could I? I haven't got any money."

Stuart turned. "How about it, Luke? You went through his pockets when you arrested him, didn't you? You find anything? Any money?"

Luke grinned wryly. "Forty-seven cents."

Stuart said: "Matt, did you see Sam Brobaker tonight?"

Matt's face turned ugly, sullen. He said: "No, by Judas, I didn't. I didn't see him. I didn't rob him. And I didn't kill him." He stared at Stuart and his eyes didn't waver.

Luke snorted—"Ha!"—and began to laugh harshly, mockingly.

Stuart asked: "Why do you hate me, Matt?"

Matt flushed and looked away. At last he mumbled: "I don't really, Stu. I guess I've always been jealous of you. I guess I've always resented the way you've fished me out of jams. But, Stu, I won't resent getting fished out of this one."

Stuart said grimly: "This isn't even your jam. It's mine."

He went out into the street and heard Luke slam and bolt the door behind him. The whole thing was getting clearer to Stuart every minute. Roark Blankenship and Norah and Stranski were all in it together. It didn't take much intelligence to figure that out. If Matt hadn't killed Sam, then Roark was lying. If Matt hadn't paid off his gambling debt, then Stranski was lying. The whole thing was a plot, a clever, diabolical plot, Stuart thought, to seize Anvil. That had to be it. Because Stranski, as tight as he was with money, would never lie himself out of $1,400 unless there was a good chance of getting back more than that.

Stuart considered for a moment what would have happened if the attempt on his life had succeeded. Anvil would have gone in equal shares to Norah and to Matt. But Matt was headed for hanging, and his share would have gone to Norah after he was hanged. Roark and Norah were apparently in love. And marriage would give Roark control of Anvil. Stranski's interest would be a silent one. And the plot would have succeeded but for one thing. Stuart himself hadn't died.

He couldn't help the chill of fear that traveled down his spine. Stuart was no coward. But how did you fight a dry-gulcher, shooting from ambush? How did you fight that, and how did you escape? The initial attempt had failed. But Stuart knew surely that they would try again. And next time they might succeed.

IV

Stuart got his horse from the rack in front of the Palace and mounted. The Palace was dark now. The crowd had dispersed from the hotel verandah, and lamps were winking out all over town. Tomorrow would be a dangerous day for Matt Dawson. Sam Brobaker had been a harmless, genial little man who was well liked and universally respected. Tonight was a dangerous night for Stuart Dawson.

Riding up Main, he could not seem to get rid of an uneasy tingle in his spine. He passed Dutch Stranski's small house at the edge of town. It was dark, but he did not pay particular attention to the fact that it was. He was too concerned with this crawling fear that made a tight knot of his stomach. Every dark clump of brush at the roadside drew his close scrutiny.

He thought he knew where Roark Blankenship would be

25

tonight. At Anvil, in Norah's arms. He thought, also, that Roark's expression when he saw him might well reveal whether or not it had been Roark who had shot him. Stuart thought it had been. But he wanted to be sure.

Suddenly, before he had gone three miles out of town, Stuart recalled the dark windows of Stranski's house. There was something wrong in that. Stuart had not been in the jail over fifteen minutes. And fifteen minutes would give Stranski enough time to close the Palace and walk home. So the lamps, if Stranski had indeed gone home, should have been lit when Stuart passed.

His fear had a solid basis in fact now, and he knew Stranski had not gone home at all. Stranski was somewhere along this road, lying in wait. Because Stuart Dawson had to be dead before the plot would work. Immediately, decisively he left the road and angled westward until he hit the creek. He put his horse into the middle of it, and followed the winding course of the creek northward toward Anvil. It was, he decided, pure folly to ride deliberately into an ambush that you knew was waiting for you. He would meet Stranski on other terms, more favorable to him, less certain for Stranski.

He felt more relaxed, now that the immediate danger had been removed, and he felt something else, too, a growing anger, and a certain pleasure in the forthcoming showdown. Yet doubt remained in his mind in spite of all this. He might prove to himself that a conspiracy existed, but how would he prove it to the sheriff, to the townspeople? He had a reputation for buying Matt out of his jams. Matt had one for getting into them. And half a dozen people had seen Matt strike him this afternoon in Stranski's. With Stranski's word that the gambling debt was paid, how would he prove otherwise? He shook his head, puzzled. And rode on.

★ ★ ★ ★ ★

Dutch Stranski crouched in the brush at the side of the road a couple of miles below Anvil's gate. Toward town, he heard the *clop-clop* of Stuart's horse, tensed, and eased the hammer on his revolver back to full cock. *Damn Roark Blankenship anyway,* he thought. If Roark had done a good job on Stuart, like he was supposed to have done, then Stranski would not have to be here now. And Matt would be blamed for the killing. This way, Stuart's death would constitute a loose end, and Stranski hated loose ends.

But Stuart's horse left the road and angled away through the brush. Stranski wondered if Stu were suspicious. He waited another ten minutes, and at last got up and eased back into the brush after his horse.

He found the animal, untied the reins from a clump of brush, and mounted. He pointed the horse toward town with a shrug of resignation, but he had not gone a hundred yards before he reined abruptly to a stop. His broad face creased into an unpleasant smile, and his eyes widened with pleasure. He chortled: "Damn! Why didn't I think of that before?"

It was made to order. Roark Blankenship and Norah were at Anvil together. It was after 1:00 in the morning. Altogether logical, then, what Stuart would think when he came home and found them together. Whether he actually thought it or not was immaterial for Stranski's purpose. All that mattered was that it be logical, that the people of the country would believe he could think it. Still grinning widely, Stranski whirled his horse and sank in his spurs. At a hard gallop, he went up the road, and later swung in at Anvil's gate.

There was a single lamp burning in the house. Stranski flung open the huge front door without knocking. Norah and Roark Blankenship were sitting together on the sofa. Closer than a man's wife and his lawyer should sit. The faces of both were guilty as they looked up.

Stranski stormed: "You damned fool, you bungled it! Stu's alive and headed here right now."

Roark grabbed for his hat. "Then I'm getting the devil out."

Stranski slammed him back down on the sofa with a blow to his chest. "You are like the devil! Now listen to me. We can still work this out, and work it so there'll be no trouble over it. Stu'll be coming in here in a few minutes. I want you to kill him as he comes in the door."

"Not me. They'll hang me for that."

"Uhn-uh. No they won't. Your story'll be that Stuart accused you of playing around with his wife and took a shot at you. You'd come out here because you wanted to try and help Matt, and you had to talk to Stu about it. But he was in a bad temper and flew off the handle. You defended yourself, that's all. I'll be your witness that there was nothing wrong going on. I'll say that I just stepped out of the room for a minute to put on some coffee, and came back in time to see him pull a gun on you. It's airtight, Roark, and you haven't any choice anyhow. Not if you want Anvil. Not if you want Norah."

Roark Blankenship's face had gone dead white. Stranski cursed inwardly. Why did he have to pick a lousy coward like Roark for a job like this? Shrugging, he knew he'd had no choice. He needed a man who was acceptable to Norah, and Roark was that.

Norah, also pale, said: "I don't like it."

Stranski felt a stab of doubt. Was Norah going soft on him now, when he needed her cold nerve the most? He asked: "Why not? You agreed that Stuart had to die. What's the matter with this way?"

She smiled. "I'm not worrying about Stuart. I'm worrying about me. This kind of a deal will ruin my reputation."

Stranski laughed with relief. "What the devil do you care

about that? You won't be staying around Castle Rock. New York was what you wanted, wasn't it? And what Roark wanted? You two were to go away, and appoint me manager at Anvil. So what difference does a reputation make?"

She shrugged, apparently convinced. "None, I guess."

"All right, then. Let's quit arguing about it. Stuart will be here in a few minutes. I'll go out in the kitchen and wait. Roark, get your gun ready. And do a job of it this time, will you?"

V

Matt Dawson lay utterly still on the bunk for a long time after Stuart had left, staring up at the ceiling. It was still a shock to him, the things that had happened tonight. And he began to sweat as he realized the seriousness of this jam he was in. Sam Brobaker had been well-liked, and the townspeople needed only a night to think things over before the shock of Sam's murder wore off and they began to get angry. Morning, Matt knew, would see a mob of them gathered around the jail, fearing that again Stuart would buy Matt out, and Sam's death would go unavenged. They'd be intent on avenging the death before that could happen. The sweat on his body turned cold and clammy. He shivered with his new, raw fear.

The sheriff sat at his desk, feet upon it, dozing. A rifle leaned against the desk at his side. Outside, the night was still, save for the occasional yip of a coyote, the occasional answering bark of a dog.

Matt struggled with himself, and gradually regained enough composure so that his brain could begin to work. And he began to put two and two together as Stuart had. In the first place, Stranski had had that watch. Matt had given it to him as security for a gambling stake, which he'd promptly lost. So it followed, then, that Stranski was behind the attempt on Stuart's life. Also, Matt knew he had not killed Sam Brobaker. Yet someone had.

And Stranski claimed Matt had paid off the balance of his gambling debt a few minutes after Sam was killed. So Stranski must be mixed up in Sam's death, too. Along with Roark Blankenship, who claimed to have seen Matt coming out of Sam's store and had to be lying.

For a while, the purpose behind the elaborate frame-up puzzled him. Until he thought of Norah, who he knew to be faithless since she had even made a play for Matt himself a year or so before. Then he thought of Roark Blankenship and Norah. He began to see it. If Stuart were dead, and Matt in jail charged with a murder for which he would surely hang, then Anvil would go to Norah. And if Roark married her, Anvil would fall into his hands. A stab of fear that was not concerned with himself shot through Matt suddenly. For he knew that tonight, Stuart was in mortal danger. The initial attempt on his life had failed. But there would be another. There had to be another. Unless Stranski and Roark were prepared to abandon their carefully constructed plan. And Matt knew they were not.

He swung his feet over the edge of the bunk and sat up. The sheriff was snoring lightly there at the desk. His forehead glistened with sweat, and his mouth hung half open. Matt thought: *I've got to get out of here. But how, how in the devil am I going to manage it?* He glanced at the window, and suddenly had his idea. He whispered hoarsely: "Sheriff. Sheriff."

Luke grunted, and stirred.

Matt whispered again: "Sheriff."

Luke's eyes came open. He saw Matt, saw Matt's feigned urgency. Matt said, trying to appear terrified: "Sheriff, someone's at the window. Blow out the lamp, quick."

The swivel chair squeaked as the sheriff came to his feet. He leaned over the desk and blew out the lamp with a sibilant breath.

Matt whispered: "Hear it, Sheriff? You've got to get me out of here."

Luke Bascomb snorted softly: "Like hell!"

Moonlight sent a shaft of brilliance through the cell's barred window. By its dull illumination Matt saw Luke's gun in his hand. He heard the jingle of Luke's keys. Luke whispered: "I'll get whoever's at the window away from there in a hurry."

His key grated in the cell's lock. He murmured urgently: "Matt, get over in the corner. Don't try anything now." He closed the cell door behind him and locked it. Then, stuffing the keys into his pocket, he went across the cell to the window.

The window was a little over six feet from the floor. Luke hooked a chair leg with his toe, and dragged it over under the window. He stepped up on it and peered through the window.

Something in Matt's mind said: *Now!* On silent, stocking feet, he went across the floor with a rush. The heel of his hand clubbed down viciously on Luke Bascomb's gun wrist, and the weapon clattered to the floor. Luke swung around, silent and surprised, and his knee came up into Matt's jaw. For an instant, the world reeled before Matt's eyes, and he staggered back. Luke jumped down and stooped to retrieve the gun. Luke thought Matt was done. But Matt's trouble was too urgent to allow him to quit. Even groggy from that knee in the jaw—even knowing that Luke would shoot when he got that gun in his hand. Matt rushed, swinging a long, looping left hook. It caught the sheriff as he was straightening, and it caught him squarely in the throat. He banged back against the wall, choking. Matt seized his gun hand and twisted viciously.

Pain and choking had relaxed Luke's muscles only slightly. But it was enough. Matt felt the hard, cold steel of the gun in his own hand. He stepped away a pace and said softly, harshly: "I've got it now, Luke. Whether you live or die depends on what you do when you catch your breath."

Luke choked: "You want the keys. They're in my right hip pocket."

Matt sat down on the edge of his bunk and carefully, one handed, he pulled on first one boot and then the other. He said: "No. I want you to take a ride with me tonight."

"It won't work, Matt. In the morning there'll be fifty men on your trail and they'll run you down. When they catch up with you, it'll be the nearest cottonwood limb for you, and I won't be able to stop them. You'd better stay here and put your trust in Stu."

"It's Stu I'm worried about. Get going, Luke. I'll tell you a few things as we ride."

Luke shrugged. "All right. I can't keep you from making a fool of yourself, I guess."

Matt grinned shakily. "No. I guess you can't. Move out, Luke."

The night air outside the jail was cool, and the town had every appearance of being alseep. Luke Bascomb's horse was tied before the jail. Matt said: "Don't yell, Luke. I'll shoot you if you do, and you can depend on that."

"I know you would, Matt. You're sorry already you broke jail, now, ain't you?"

Matt shook his head. "Where can I get a horse?"

Luke was silent, grinning. Matt looked at the sheriff's horse, and decided the animal was big enough to carry them both. At least as far as Anvil. He said: "All right, get up, but no tricks." He held the horse's left rein in his own hand until the sheriff had mounted. Then he put a hand on the horn and swung up behind, first shoving the gun into his belt.

Mounted, he took it out again and dug the muzzle into the sheriff's back. His heels drummed on the horse's ribs. The animal didn't like riding double, but he moved out away from the jail without bucking. And at the edge of town, Matt kicked

him into a gallop. As he rode, he talked. Not because he thought he would be believed. But only because Luke Bascomb had to be filled in on the things that were happening so that when he saw what Matt hoped he would see, he would not be confused, but would, at last, accept the truth of what he saw. Matt held the horse at a steady lope, praying that time was not too short.

As they turned in at Anvil's gate, Matt, who had been silent for a full three miles, said softly: "Luke, I'm going to forget about holding the gun on you, if you'll promise to see this through. In return, I'll promise to go back with you if I'm wrong. How about it?"

Luke shrugged. "You really believe this yarn, don't you?"

"You're blamed right I believe it." But Matt was beginning to wonder. He was beginning to wonder if all of his thinking had not been wishful, the hopefulness of desperation.

Luke muttered: "Well, all right. But give me back the gun, Matt. I don't want anybody else getting shot."

Matt hesitated. Finally he handed the gun forward to Luke. They dismounted in the yard, making every effort to be quiet. A single lamp burned inside the house. Elsewhere, everything was dark and still.

The sheriff hesitated there in the yard with the gun in his hand. Matt reminded softly—"Luke, you promised."—and at last Bascomb shrugged. "All right. Play out the hand. What are we supposed to do now?"

"There's a window around the corner, facing on the porch. There's a lot of vines there, so we'll be in the shadow and Stu won't see us when he comes in."

Carefully, silently the two tiptoed up onto the porch and around the corner. They came to the window and looked inside. Matt saw Norah on the sofa, saw Roark Blankenship beside her. Between them, silent and deadly, lay Roark's gun.

Matt looked at the sheriff's face. He said: "See how white

and nervous they both are? See that gun? Do you believe me now?"

He heard a horse come into the yard. Looking out through the climbing vines, he saw a horseman riding up from the creek. But Stuart did not ride to the porch and dismount. Neither did he take his horse to the corral. He dismounted in the middle of the yard and went at a swift and silent run to the kitchen door.

Matt whispered: "Judas. He knows what's going on. And I'll bet you ten to one that Stranski's in the kitchen. Luke, we've got to do something."

Before Luke could protest, Matt crossed the porch, letting his boots scrape noisily. And put his hand on the doorknob and flung it open.

VI

Stuart's observing eyes did not miss the sheriff's horse, wandering loose in the yard. Neither did they miss Roark Blankenship's livery stable horse tied near the porch and Stranski's horse cropping grass from the fence line nearby. He ran silently to the kitchen door, grinning just a little because men laying an ambush ought to plan it carefully enough to hide their horses. But the sheriff's horse puzzled him. He began to wonder if the sheriff was in this, too.

On the stoop before the kitchen door, he paused long enough to remove his boots and draw his gun. Then he stepped into the kitchen. He must have made some slight noise on the stoop, because Stranski was waiting for him. He felt the gambler's presence even as he pulled the door to behind him. He felt it and whirled, dodging.

Stranski whispered: "Stu, I've been waiting for you."

"Why? What the devil are you doing up here?" He was vastly puzzled. He had expected an attack from Stranski, and this whispered talk was unnerving.

"I think there's something going on between Roark and your wife."

Stuart laughed sarcastically: "And if there was, what damned business would it be of yours? Get out of here, Stranski, before I kill you."

He heard a shot bellow in the front room, and sprang toward the door, conscious of Stranski behind him but unable to wait now. He asked himself even as he burst through the kitchen door: *What the devil? Norah?* Roark Blankenship stood beside the sofa, and there was a smoking gun in his hand. Norah screamed. Matt stood in the front doorway, his hands empty, a look of shocked surprise on his face.

Stuart said: "Roark. Turn around. Shoot at me."

Roark's expression of surprise was almost ludicrous. He stared at Stuart, then back at Matt, who was swaying now, turning white in the face.

Stranski's gun prodded viciously into Stuart's back. "Drop it, Stu. Drop it, or I'll blow your guts out."

Stuart let his gun clatter to the floor. Stranski began to chuckle nervously. "All right, Roark. Kill him now. And do a good job of it. We're still in the clear. Our story is still good. Matt's the only complication and he'll be easily enough explained. He's escaped from jail, an accused murderer. Nobody'll blame us for killing him." As he spoke, he stepped aside, out of the line of fire. Roark raised his gun.

Stuart knew he was staring at death now. He tore his glance from the gaping gun muzzle in Roark's hand and looked at Norah. She was pale as death, but she made no move to stop this execution. Her eyes met his glance, and then dropped away. He said sourly: "What you want you want bad, don't you, Norah?" He looked at the wavering gun in Roark's hand, at the tightening, downward turn of the corners of his mouth. And he looked over at Matt.

35

Matt's glance had flicked to the window. Stuart followed his glance and saw the sheriff peering in. Then the sheriff was gone, and Stuart guessed he was coming around to the door. But whether he was in this, or only after Matt, there would be no time for him to intervene. Only split seconds of life were left. Stuart thought: *I'm not standing here to be shot down like a dog. I'll at least wreck their plan if I can.* He dived for his gun on the floor. The gun in Roark Blankenship's hand bellowed, deafening in the closed confines of the room. Acrid, black powder smoke billowed from the gun muzzle. Stuart got his hand on the gun. But another gun roared behind him, and something slammed against his arm. The gun dropped from his nerveless fingers. He rolled and grabbed at the gun with his left hand. Groping, fumbling, shocked by the bullet that had torn into his right arm, he turned and glanced upward at Roark.

At that instant, Matt's hurtling body took Roark's legs out from under him, and Norah's, and the three of them collapsed in a pile on the floor. Matt was fighting for Roark's gun, fighting, clawing, making throaty sounds like a savage and wounded animal. And Stranski, behind him, lost his head completely. He fired blindly into the tangle of bodies there on the floor. Stuart couldn't see what he hit, if anything. Because he was rolling again, trying to bring his gun to bear on Stranski. He tried to raise himself a little on the wounded right arm so that he could fire. But the arm had no strength. He lay back, and tried to bring the gun into line. From out of the tangle of bodies on the floor before the sofa, a gun barked. Stranski seemed frozen for an instant. Then, slowly, his gun lowered until its muzzle was pointing at the floor. His knees wobbled, and collapsed, and he fell in a heap, unmoving.

The sheriff burst through the door, gun in hand. But Stuart was up, driving toward the pile before the sofa. And Matt was grinning up at him weakly from there. Stuart put a hand down

36

to help Matt up. Norah was lying across Matt's legs, an inert weight. Her face was waxen, her breathing stilled. And Roark Blankenship had fainted from fear. The sheriff pushed both Matt and Stuart down onto the sofa. Now the crew came streaming through the door to collect in a group before it, dazed and shocked by the carnage. Luke Bascomb gave them crisp, terse orders, even as he cut the sleeve away from Stuart's arm wound, the pants away from Matt's leg wound.

Stuart looked at Matt, and Matt made a light grin. There was something strange in Matt's eyes, a kind of waiting. Stuart said: "Matt, thanks. I'd have been a dead pigeon. . . ."

That seemed to be what Matt had been waiting for. His grin widened and he said weakly: "You said something about a job on Anvil." He was fighting the weakness that tried to claim his consciousness.

Bascomb growled: "Shut up, the both of you."

Stuart said: "Yeah, Matt. Sure." His left hand went out and squeezed Matt's arm. He was seeing things this moment that he had never been able to see before. Matt had only needed to feel strong and important, something neither Lucky nor Stuart or his mother had ever allowed him. But he was all right now. He'd fished Stuart out of Stuart's jam, and it was all he needed. Stuart lay back and let the lassitude of his wound claim him.

★ ★ ★ ★ ★

LONE RIDER

★ ★ ★ ★ ★

I

At noon they stopped and dismounted, and ate cold sliced beef and cold sourdough biscuits. Without seeming to, Lew Stark watched J.W., who had raised him from a pup, missing neither the weariness that was in the older man nor the pallor that must be caused by his persistent, hacking cough.

J.W.'s hand trembled as he tipped the canteen to wash down the last of his meal. It was frailer, more transparent than it had been a year ago. There was something different in the old man's eyes, and that hadn't been there a year ago, either. It had happened last winter when J.W. Regal's four sons had come to him and threatened to take the .45 Ranch out of his hands, claiming he was senile and unable to manage it himself.

Old J.W. Regal had hacked the .45 out of Comanche land. He'd built it steadily over the last twenty-five years of his life, and now the .45 was the biggest ranch within a hundred miles. Maybe they could do it and maybe they couldn't. Lew didn't know. But he did know he'd give them the damnedest fight they'd ever had if they tried it. He'd seen what the threat had done to J.W. It had put a quiet terror into his pale old eyes, and Lew had never seen fear in them before. It had made J.W. crowd himself far beyond the limits of his endurance, proving that they were wrong.

The cough, which had hung on too long, really didn't surprise Lew. But it worried him, worried him constantly. Damn them, anyway. J.W. was no more senile than he was. But Ira Regal was

41

a lawyer, and Ira might just make it stick. Either that or he'd drive the old man to collapse with worry over it.

Lew rolled a smoke and J.W. lit a thin cigar. For a few moments they sat on the ground in companionable silence. At last, J.W. got stiffly to his feet. He said: "You ride over to Comanche Springs and see how many bulls are there. I'll go to the salt lick on Buffalo Hump. Meet you back here in two, three hours."

Lew protested: "Damn it, I can check Comanche Springs and Buffalo Hump, too. Why don't you go on back home? I'll see you there tonight."

"And let them say I'm getting old . . . let them say I'm senile? To hell with that." He grinned then, and gripped Lew's shoulder. "I'm all right. I'm as tough as I ever was."

Lew said: "Sure you are. All right. See you later." He swung to his horse and rode away.

He looked back from the first rise. J.W. was riding at a steady trot toward Buffalo Hump, a long, hog-backed ridge seven or eight miles away. Lew grinned ruefully. Maybe he was worrying unnecessarily. Maybe the old man *was* all right. But he didn't quite convince himself.

He rode steadily for a little more than an hour. He found three of J.W.'s new Hereford bulls at Comanche Springs, and they seemed to be in good shape. Satisfied, he started back.

Since noon, clouds had been rolling up from the mountains in the west, black, heavy clouds that were now shedding rain like a gray curtain as they swept along. Lew gigged his horse into a lope. He hadn't brought a slicker and neither had J.W. And there was no shelter anywhere closer than Mike Santoyo's shack.

Half an hour later, the rain struck, slanting sharply out of the southwest, driven on by a gale-size wind. In minutes, Lew was soaked to the hide. Then it began to hail.

He ducked his head against the pea-size stones. His horse,

stung, crow-hopped a couple of times and then began to run. Water pouring down dry watercourses formed sluggish, mud-laden floods. Hail floated along on the water. The stones increased in size until they were as big as marbles and almost as hard. The air chilled rapidly.

A single hailstone, almost the size of an egg, decided the issue. "To hell with this!" Lew growled, and reined over to head for Mike Santoyo's, knowing J.W. would do the same.

This was the southeast part of the new State of Colorado. These two hundred thousand acres of waving grass and rolling land had, not twenty years before, held the great, wild herds of buffalo, the villages of Comanches and Cheyennes. Now it held cattle, reds, blacks, brindles, and roans, all bearing the .45 brand on their hips. These were the descendants of Texas cattle, almost as wild as buffalo, almost as fleet as deer. J.W.'s two hundred Hereford bulls had yet to make their mark upon the herd.

The ever-present worry about J.W. touched Lew as he rode. J.W. Regal was past the age when a soaking meant no more than discomfort and inconvenience. Getting soaked and chilled could mean serious sickness to J.W. He was past seventy and he had that damned, persistent cough.

There was a covering of hailstones on the ground by the time Lew reached Santoyo's shack. His shoulders and back were bruised and tender from the pelting of the hail. His hat was smashed flat. The hand that held the reins was puffy and swelling from repeated blows of icy hail. He slid blindly to a halt before Santoyo's squat house, dismounted, and led his horse under the overhang of the rude porch roof.

Streaming water, thoroughly chilled, battered, and irritable, he stared out for a moment at the deluge, awed by its fury, awed by the thunderous sound it made on Mike's tin roof. Then he turned toward the door, wondering why it had not already opened. It was then that he became aware of the fight inside. He heard a muffled curse, heard the solid thump of something hitting the flimsy frame wall of the shack.

He seized the door pull and yanked it forward. The room was a shambles. Natalia Santoyo, her clothes half torn from her body, one side of her face flaming with the imprint of a hand, was struggling with a man on the far side of the room. Mike Santoyo was not present.

Lew's surprise passed quickly, to be replaced by raw, unthinking fury. Natalia Santoyo was seventeen, and she was like a sister to him. She'd practically been raised at the .45, and to Lew she was still only a young girl. Besides, in Lew's book, only the lowest of men would force a woman against her will.

His voice was sharp and harsh, filled with raging disgust. "Roma! Get your filthy hands off her!"

Roma released Natalia as though she had burned his hands. He whirled, hand darting toward the gun at his side. But it wasn't there. It lay on the floor at Lew's feet, where it had fallen during Roma's struggle with Natalia.

Lew said softly, viciously: "I just wish you had it, you son-of-a-bitch."

Alameda Roma. A big, raw brute of a man, son of an Irish washerwoman at Fort Alameda, Arizona. The Roma name came from his Mexican father, who had briefly lived with his mother, and then gone on. The boy was born and raised without him, his only heritage a bitter hatred for all Mexicans.

Roma stared almost blankly at Lew for a moment, passion for Natalia quickly changing into a current of frustration directed at Lew.

Natalia, more furious than scared, spoke in a voice laden with disgust: "Let him go, Lew. Just let him get out of here so I won't have to look at him."

"No! By God, no! When he goes, he'll crawl."

"Lew!"

He looked at her. If he'd needed anything to spur his fury, he got it in that single glance. One of her shoulders was bare, and upon it were the marks of Roma's teeth. He lunged across the room. His mind was almost dumb with rage. His mouth opened and he heard his own voice, strange and savagely tight: "Animal! You dirty god-damn' animal!"

Roma side-stepped, avoiding Lew, and as Lew went past, he brought his huge right fist down like a maul. It struck Lew's head and grazed the side of his face, nearly tearing loose an ear. In excruciating pain, Lew slammed into the wall like a blind steer hitting a fence, and the whole building shook with the impact. A couple of dishes on an overhanging shelf came crashing down to shatter over his head.

Roma was crossing the room, his eyes on the revolver that had dropped from his holster during the struggle with Natalia. Lew dived after him. He hit Roma from behind as Roma stooped for the gun. His body struck with an impact that drove Roma against the door. The combined impact of their bodies splintered the door, smashed its flimsy panels. They plunged on through and rolled in the damp dirt of the sheltered porch area outside.

Lew's horse snorted shrilly. He shied away from the shelter and into the streaming, pelting storm. Dragging reins, eyes rolling wildly, he lunged around toward the rear of the shack. Roma rolled, scrambling, and kneed Lew in the face as he got up. Lew felt blood spout from his nose. He drove forward and up, and felt his head slam into Roma's mid-section like a ram.

Roma grunted and staggered back, his legs pumping furiously to keep himself erect. When he struck the slick clay mud at the edge of the porch, they failed him. He fell back heavily into mud and water and accumulated hailstones, raising a monstrous spray of water and sliding a full four feet. Lew, on hands and knees, lunged up. Running, he dived at Roma. He landed with both knees on the man's chest and thought he felt, or heard over the roar of the storm, the cracking of ribs beneath them. Roma rolled and slipped away, covered with mud, elusive as an eel. Lew tried to follow, but the slimy footing betrayed him. His feet slid out from under him and he went down, face first, in the mud.

He spat mud from his mouth on a stream of invective. He wiped a sleeve across his face and stood in the streaming rain, looking around for his opponent. Hailstones battered him but he didn't feel them. Rain streamed into his face, washing the mud and blood away. Roma had lunged back into the porch's shelter. He crossed it, shambling like a great, enraged bear, and seized a weathered oak singletree that hung from a rusty nail on the cabin wall. A great, knotted hand clasped each of its ends. Held thus, it was infinitely more dangerous than if held as a club, for it prevented Lew from getting past it to the man behind.

Lew scarcely saw the weapon. He charged in out of the rain, crossed the porch toward Roma like an enraged bull. In his ears at the moment of impact was Natalia's terror-stricken scream. He saw the singletree coming up. It struck him in the chest and for an instant he was sure his chest had collapsed. The weight of his charge had knocked Roma against the cabin wall. One of the man's hands went back as he fought for balance, leaving the singletree dangling from the other.

Lew struggled to breathe, gasping, choking, at the moment completely helpless. Roma swung the singletree, his face bloody, his lips curled back from his fine white teeth in a concentrated snarl. Lew hunched and the thing grazed his left shoulder and came up hard against the side of his head, only part of its force lost. Sideways he fell, kept erect only by the cabin wall, which he struck with a thump. He clung to it, his senses fading, and watched Roma come toward him, murder in his tiny eyes, the singletree raised like a club straight over his head and a little behind it.

At that instant, Lew could do nothing to protect himself. He was done, finished, dead, if that singletree came down and struck his head. Chance saved him. Chance alone. There was not enough clearance for the club to swing. It struck the porch roof as Roma brought it forward. The expression on Roma's face was one of almost ludicrous surprise. Thrown off balance by the unexpected resistance the singletree encountered, he ducked, and finished the swing lamely, with little force. Lew pushed himself sideways, reached out, and seized the club as it came down. Roma yanked, and splinters dug into Lew's hands as the singletree slid through them. But he held on, and was pulled forward.

Roma swung him, as though he were a dog with a rag in its jaws. Lew was flung across the porch, half running, but he held grimly to the singletree as though life depended upon not letting go, and when he reached the end of the swing, his weight tore the club from Roma's hands.

Roma immediately looked around the porch, searching for some other weapon. Lew staggered out into the full fury of the storm and fell in the mud. All along the wall equipment was hanging. There was a double set of weathered wagon harness. There were several halters and bridles and an old, beat-up saddle. And there was something else, a rusty double-bitted axe with a weathered, splintered handle.

Roma yanked it down. Natalia came running desperately across the porch, swinging a heavy black iron skillet. Roma struck it from her hands, then cuffed her, hard, on the side of the head. She staggered against the wall, dazed. Lew came out of the rain. His eyes were tiny bits of gray slate, as murderous as the ends of bullets staring out of a revolver cylinder. His mouth was a thin, straight line. Blood and mud covered him from hair to scuffed boots. But he held the singletree as Roma had held it, one hand at each end.

Roma rushed, swinging the axe in a vicious arc. Lew backed away, careful of the mud now, careful not to lose his footing, and the axe whistled harmlessly through empty air a foot from his chest. Roma's eyes were completely without sanity. Lew knew that if he made one misstep, one mistake, Roma would literally hack him to pieces with the axe. As wary as a wolf, he circled, forcing Roma to lead. And Roma, out of his head with fury and pain, brought the axe over his head and down with force enough to split a foot-thick block of cedar. Lew, unable to step back, parried with the singletree.

The axe struck. Lew's hands, holding the singletree, turned numb with the shock of it. His shoulders felt as though they were being torn from their sockets. And he heard a splintering noise. For an instant, both men were still, frozen there in the pelting hail and rain. The sound of the hail on the roof was like the roll of a thousand drums; the sound of running water was like that of a flood.

Roma held a splintered axe handle in his two hands. He stared at it stupidly. He looked down at his boots. The axe head was buried almost halfway in one of them. Lew didn't look that far. He saw that the axe was broken and it was all he needed. Dropping the singletree, he lunged at Roma. He tore the axe handle out of Roma's hands and flung it fifty feet away. And then he went to work.

His fists beat against Roma's craggy face like pistons in a steam threshing machine. He drove the man back and down, and still he pounded, the way a man will sometimes pound a snake that is dead but that is still unbelievably evil and repulsive. They rolled from high ground to low until they were half buried in water. Then Lew's blows lost their force because of the resisting power of the water in which they landed.

Bubbles rose from Roma's nose. Lew seized his hair, yanked up his head, and watched him gasp life-giving air. Then, holding Roma's hair in a bleeding left fist, he smashed his right with all the force of which it was capable into Roma's mouth. Roma's head dropped back into the slime.

Vaguely he heard a man's shouting voice and the screams of a woman. Then he felt hands tugging at his shredded shirt. And finally he heard the deafening concussion of a gun, fired right beside his ear. He surged to his feet, swinging, battle in his eyes. He saw old J.W. Regal standing there, a smoking pistol in his aged fist.

J.W. screeched over the roar of the storm: "Enough! That's enough! He's half dead now!"

Lew looked at him stupidly. The red haze of fury was slow to fade from his mind. His head swung ponderously and he looked at Natalia, cowering on the porch. He turned back to Roma, whose head was submerged in muddy water. Stooping, he grabbed Roma's booted feet and dragged the man out of the puddle. Roma gasped like a fish on a dry bank. But he was alive.

Lew turned and staggered toward the porch, a little awed and frightened by the intensity of his own terrible rage. Today, for the first time in his life, he had wanted to kill. And he almost had.

II

J.W. Regal was a little farther from Santoyo's than Lew was when the storm began, and he traveled somewhat more slowly and cautiously than Lew. So he was nearly twenty minutes behind Lew in arriving. Like Lew, he was soaked to the skin, battered and bruised by the hailstones. He was shivering violently as he rode into sight of the shack. His lips were blue and his loose false teeth rattled like castanets.

He saw Lew and Alameda Roma fighting in the mud and water before the shack, saw Natalia cowering on the porch. He saw Roma seize the axe, knock Natalia aside, and rush at Lew. He spurred his horse and yanked his rifle from its saddle boot. The horse slipped and slid down the slope, nearly fell, recovered, and then came to a stiff-legged halt beside the porch.

J.W. swung down, colder than he had ever been before. He raised the rifle, intending to shoot Roma before he'd let the man kill Lew, but the muzzle wavered so violently he knew he'd never be able to hit the man. Anger at himself, at this growing helplessness within himself, rose in him. He flung the rifle aside angrily and drew his revolver.

Natalia stared at him beseechingly from the ground beneath the porch roof, like a frightened little girl. But she didn't look like a girl. She was soaking wet from spray, and her clothes clung to her body, the body of a woman, not of a girl.

J.W. thumbed back the hammer on his pistol and ran toward Lew and Roma. He saw the axe rise and it fell so quickly he had no time to raise and aim his gun. He heard the axe handle splinter on Lew's parrying singletree.

He began to grin bleakly as he watched Lew fling aside the singletree and wrench the splintered axe handle from Roma's hands. He stepped in under the porch roof, holstering his gun as he did.

A look at Natalia's torn blouse told him what the fight was about. He saw the red mark of Roma's hand on her face, the marks of Roma's teeth in her bare shoulder. The same fury that had risen in Lew at the sight now rose in J.W. Natalia was the closest thing he had to a daughter. He thought of her as a daughter. Her father was his closest friend. So he watched while Lew beat Roma back, beat him down to the ground, almost beat him into it. And only when it appeared certain Lew would kill the man, did he intervene.

Stopping Lew was not easy. And the look on Lew's face as he turned awed the old man and made a cold chill of foreboding run down his spine. Because he remembered another time, another man. He remembered Lew's father wearing the same twisted expression of ungovernable rage that Lew now wore.

Oh, God, would Lew travel the same route his father had? J.W. had prayed these many years that he'd never see in Lew the things that had made a killer out of his father so many years before. Now he was seeing those things. Now, at this tiny shack in the streaming rain, the temper that had remained hidden in Lew these many years had at last come to the fore.

And then it was gone. Lew looked at him worriedly and said: "For God's sake, J.W., get inside the house. You're blue with cold."

An odd feeling of relief came over J.W. at the change in Lew. Perhaps he'd been wrong. Perhaps he hadn't seen what he'd thought he'd seen at all. Hell, anyone would get mad at what Roma had tried to do. And yet, somewhere within himself, he knew, even as he turned toward the house, that he'd made no mistake. The wildness, the ungovernable temper that had made Ace Stark an outlaw and killer were present in his son. J.W. hoped, with quiet desperation, that circumstances would never arise that would bring them out again.

Lew followed J.W. toward the house. Natalia preceded them inside. She hurried into the bedroom and returned with a blanket around her bare shoulders. She looked steadily at Lew for a moment before she said: "Take him into the bedroom, Lew, and get those wet clothes off him. He's half frozen. There are some of Father's things in there he can put on. I'll make coffee."

J.W. grumbled, but he went into the bedroom readily enough and began to strip off his soggy clothes. Natalia opened the door enough to admit her hand and flung in a couple of towels.

51

Lew stripped and toweled himself vigorously. He found a couple of pairs of Mike Santoyo's pants, gave J.W. one and put one on himself. J.W. was still shivering. His thin, muscular body jumped and twitched. Lew found him a wool plaid shirt and J.W. put it on. Lew said: "Get on out there by the stove."

"You'll have to do something about Roma," J.W. said.

"To hell with him." Lew's mouth was hard.

J.W. said: "That axe head went into his foot."

Lew's eyes widened with surprise. "Bad?"

"Looked bad. We'd better tie it up. We don't want him to bleed to death."

Lew stooped, put on his soggy socks and sodden boots. Shirtless, he left the room and went outside. Hurrying, wincing against the pelting rain, he crossed to Roma, got him under the shoulders, and dragged him to the porch.

Roma's boot was split open. It left a red trail in the mud and water as Lew dragged him along. Lew laid him down and reëntered the house. Out of his sodden pants he got his jackknife. He went back outside and cut the boot from Roma's foot. After that, he cut away the sock.

Roma's foot was split, cloven like the hoof of a cow. It flowed blood steadily. Roma's face was gray as death.

No pity stirred in Lew's face. He went back into the house. "I need some towels, or something for bandages."

Natalia silently brought him several. He returned outside and, kneeling, tied up Roma's foot. The blood hadn't spurted, so there probably was no artery cut. Roma could make it back to town.

Lew went around the house, caught Roma's horse and his own, and led them back to the porch. He tied them and went inside. "Has Mike got any whiskey?"

Natalia brought him a brown bottle. He went out and, kneeling again, raised Roma's head and poured whiskey into his mouth. Roma choked and coughed and opened his eyes. They were flat with pain.

Lew said: "I'll help you mount."

Roma's eyes cleared. They hated Lew silently, virulently.

Lew said evenly: "If I ever see you on Forty-Five again, I'll kill you."

Roma didn't answer. He struggled to his feet, flinging off Lew's hands furiously. Lew untied Roma's horse and led him to the man. Roma snatched the reins and awkwardly fought his way into the saddle. As he hit it, his face turned ghastly. He looked at Lew and said matter-of-factly: "I'll get you, you son-of-a-bitch. I will."

He tottered there for a moment, then turned and rode out into the lessening rain at a walk, his hurt foot dangling. He headed north, toward town.

Lew watched until he was out of sight. Then he turned and went back inside.

Natalia was crying now, almost silently. Her shoulders shook as she stood before the range.

Lew crossed to her. The top of her head came to the middle of his chest. Her hair was wet and clung to her head like the fur of an otter emerging from a pond. He put his big hands on her shoulders, applying a gentle pressure. "Easy now. Easy. It's over. He won't be back."

She turned her head and looked at him gratefully. Her eyes were dark and soft and filled with tears. Her full mouth made a tremulous smile.

He was struck again, as he had been so many times before, by the sweetness in her face, in the gentle curve of her mouth and cheek. She stared up at him and gradually the smile on her mouth faded. Something passed between them and then she lowered her glance. Her face flushed faintly. She said: "The coffee's hot."

Lew dropped his hands and stepped away. But he kept his eyes on her, an awareness of her in him that had not been there before. He turned and caught J.W. watching him, a fondly indulgent smile on his face that vaguely embarrassed Lew.

He crossed the room, conscious suddenly that his chest was bare. He went into the bedroom and found another of Mike Santoyo's shirts. He put it on and returned to the other room.

He sat down at the table and sipped the scalding coffee Natalia put before him. He glanced at her, thinking that if he'd arrived a few minutes later. . . . Anger rose in him like a flood. He fought it down deliberately. Scowling, he stared at the steam arising from his cup.

Lew was tall and slim, a mild-mannered and easygoing man— usually. His gray eyes were quiet. His face, weathered by sun and prairie wind, normally wore the faintest of amiable smiles. His hair was black and crisp and coarse. It fell now in a damp, curling lock across his forehead. He'd never managed to get rid of that stubborn, boyish cowlick in the back.

J.W. had raised him. Lew couldn't remember anything before J.W. His questions about the past had always been met with evasion. So he'd eventually quit asking questions about the past. The present was good enough.

Twenty-five years before, J.W. had brought him north out of Texas, driving a herd of a thousand Texas cows. They'd settled here, on .45, in a spot where you kicked arrowheads out of the dust every now and then, where the evidences of an old Indian encampment were plainly visible.

A year passed. Then one day J.W. had ridden away toward Denver. and when he returned, he was driving a buckboard with a woman up on the seat beside him. She had lived long enough to bear him four strong sons. And then, in a bitter winter, she had sickened and died. Yet, in spite of the sons, in spite of another, younger woman who came later, the closeness never evaporated between J.W. Regal and young Lew Stark. It was as though Lew were his real son and the others foster sons he had only taken to raise.

J.W. still shivered beside Lew. Lew looked at him worriedly. Seventy was old when you'd lived the way J.W. had. Seventy was a man's allotted span.

The rain had almost ceased now, but the air was still filled with the trickling sound of water running off the roof, with the dull roar of the arroyo full of water to the banks that passed a couple of hundred yards from the house.

Lew studied J.W.'s face. The customary twinkle was gone from J.W.'s wise blue eyes. His mouth was a thin, straight line beneath his nose that, Lew had often thought, could have belonged to one of the dispossessed Cheyennes. His cheeks, covered with gray stubble, were slightly hollow beneath high cheekbones.

Lew got up and found the brown bottle he'd used to revive Roma. He poured a generous slug into J.W.'s coffee.

J.W. grinned up at him, then gulped the coffee down. Gradually his color began to return, but he kept watching Lew in an odd and worried way.

Lew looked at Natalia. "What was Roma doing here?"

"Asking questions."

"What kind of questions?"

"About Forty-Five. How big a crew you have, what kind of title you have to your range, how many cattle are on it, where the boundaries are."

Lew grinned. "What'd you tell him?"

Natalia grinned back. "I told him to go to the devil."

Lew glanced at J.W. He said: "I've met Roma in town. Claims to be a cattleman. He approached me about leasing range. Said he had three thousand cattle on the way here from Texas, and needed grass for them. I told him no."

He heard suddenly the sucking sounds of a horse's hoofs outside in the mud. He got to his feet and went to the door. He flung it open.

Mike Santoyo, dripping like a drowned rat, was dismounting just beyond the overhang of the porch roof. He tied his horse under it, then crossed to the door.

He was short, wiry, and dark-skinned as a Comanche. Dressed in buckskins and quill-decorated moccasins, he had a wild, gamy look to him that matched his smell, essence of wet buckskin, old campfire smoke, and rancid animal grease. His teeth flashed in a white smile that managed to be both cordial and fierce. "Horse throw you, Lew?"

Lew backed from the door. As he came in, Santoyo took off the floppy, wide-brimmed hat he wore, and shook a shower of water from his long black hair. His saturated buckskins clung to him like skin, but he didn't seem to be cold or even uncomfortable.

Lew said: "Yeah. My horse fell." He glanced at Natalia to see if this deception was what she wanted. Her eyes told him it was. She knew old Mike better even than Lew did. If Mike knew about Roma, Roma would turn up within a week with his throat cut. Probably scalped as well. And the knife work would point the finger straight at Mike.

Mike's eyes were black as shoe buttons and as expressionless. "Cut yourself, Lew?"

Lew's look was blank for the barest instant.

Mike said: "Blood outside on the ground. A lot of blood." He looked around at the disordered room. "Who'd you fight?"

Lew resigned himself. "All right. It was that stranger from Medicine Lodge. Roma. He was pawing Natalia."

Mike's eyes glittered.

Lew said quickly: "He got what was coming to him, Mike. You let him alone."

J.W. put in: "He's got a cloven hoof from your double-bitted axe, Mike. Let him alone. He's had enough."

Mike turned and looked at J.W. Immediately his eyes filled with concern, but he didn't say anything. He reached over and picked up the brown bottle from the table. He poured J.W.'s cup half full, then dumped a generous portion into a glass for himself.

J.W. drank it, shivering again.

Lew studied Mike Santoyo. An instant before he had been fierce, dangerous. There had been murder in his glittering eyes. Now his face was soft as a woman's. He said: "J.W., you're a damned old fool. You're seventy years old and you act like fifteen. Why don't you let Lew and them four no-account sons of yours run Forty-Five? Why don't you stay in out of the god-damned weather once in a while?"

"I'm all right," said J.W. with gruff resentment.

"Oh, hell yes. You're all right. You're shivering like a dog passing peach seeds, but you're all right. Lew, take him home. Pour a pint down him and put him to bed. If the damned old goat won't use his head, somebody'll have to do his thinking for him."

J.W. scowled, but there was a lurking warmth in his eyes. "Who's an old goat? You ain't so god-damned young yourself."

Natalia spoke sharply, her eyes twinkling: "Stop it, you two! Lew, I think Mike is right. J.W. ought to be in bed."

Lew nodded. Natalia went into the bedroom and came back with a ragged sheepskin. J.W. protested, but he put it on.

Lew looked down at Mike as he stood by the door, waiting for J.W. to button the coat. He said: "Let Roma alone, Mike. He's not worth hanging for. Besides, I told him if I ever saw him on Forty-Five again, *I'd* kill him."

Mike glanced at Natalia, then back to Lew. He neither agreed nor disagreed. Lew knew it was the best he could do. You didn't tell Mike Santoyo what to do. He did as he pleased, had as long as Lew could remember. He belonged to a dying breed. He'd been an Indian trader, a beaver trapper, a scout, a hunter. He'd given up each of his colorful occupations as progress killed them off. Now he sold wolves' ears to J.W. Regal. Ears from wolves killed on .45. And occasionally he got a lion. J.W. paid him $5 a pair for wolves' ears, $25 for the hide of a lion. It was a good deal for both of them. J.W. saved more in calves than he paid Mike. And Mike made a living for himself and Natalia without changing his way of life, without leaving this shack.

Lew grinned to himself, remembering the first time he'd seen Mike. Mike had been living in a buffalo-hide teepee, right here on this very spot. He'd had an Arapaho squaw. She had died when Lew was ten, and for a couple of years Mike lived alone. Then he'd married a Spanish woman in Santa Fe and brought her here to live. She had refused to live in an Indian lodge, so Mike had built the shack.

Apparently the Spanish woman hadn't liked the shack much better than the lodge, for she'd stayed only long enough to bear Natalia and then had gone off with a Mexican shepherd who had been passing through with a flock. Natalia, a squalling, red-faced brat, had come to .45 to live. And she'd stayed there until she was eight. Then she'd gone, filled with a touching childish sense of responsibility, to keep house for Mike.

J.W. finished buttoning the coat and looked at Lew irritably. "Well, if you're going to baby me, you'd just as well get started."

The old asperity was in his eyes as he spoke, but Lew knew it was sham. J.W. was still shaking with chills. J.W. was a very sick man.

III

The rain had stopped altogether by the time they stepped out the door. They mounted and set out toward home. The ride, which normally would have taken less than an hour, took three because of the flooded condition of the land. Dry arroyos that Lew had never seen running water were almost full to the banks today. Débris and white foam rolled along on the thick, muddy surfaces. The footing was bad for horses. They floundered and scrambled, falling several times.

J.W. finished the ride hanging onto his saddle horn, a thing Lew had never seen him do before. His teeth were rattling, his lips and chin quivering. And now his face was slightly flushed.

The ranch looked like a fort, and indeed that was what it had been when J.W. built it nearly twenty-five years before. It had adobe walls fifteen feet high, topped with shards of broken glass. The ponderous gates lay sagging against the inside walls. The hardware had rusted off and had never been replaced, for there was, by that time, no further need for gates. But inside, it was exactly like a fort. Individual rooms had been built against the walls, and were joined by a covered gallery that ran all the way around. At the far end, a house had been built, also of adobe. It ran the full width of the enclosure, its walls formed by the outer walls of the fort on two sides and in the rear.

Once, J.W. had corralled his stock inside at night. Now there was a bunkhouse and cook shack, an adobe barn, a corral, and a blacksmith shop standing to the left of the fort-like structure. There were two gigantic cottonwoods inside the walls, and a little patch of lawn.

Rafael, thirteen-year-old son of Ortiz, the chore man, took the horses as Lew and J.W. dismounted. J.W. stumbled on the edge of the brick-paved gallery, and staggered. Lew caught his arm.

He looked at J.W.'s flushed face with alarm. Damn it, sickness shouldn't come on this fast. But, he remembered, J.W. had been coughing for a week. The storm and chilling had probably only aggravated what he already had. The trouble was, J.W. was old, whether he liked admitting it or not. He didn't have the resistance or strength of a younger man.

J.W. flung off Lew's arm irritably. He opened the door and stepped inside. Lew followed.

The living room was almost fifty feet long, and more than half that wide. Furniture was mostly homemade, of cedar and pine, pegged together laboriously and strung with rawhide to support the cushions. Leona Regal rose from one of the sofas as they entered, looking younger than her thirty-five years. She crossed the room to them, her eyes touching J.W., and then passing on to Lew, where they lingered, brightening.

Leona was tall for a woman, and made with the statuesque proportions of a Venus. She was clad today in simple red-and-white-checked gingham, which did not particularly suit her. It made her look simple and domestic, and she was neither. The personal quality of her glance embarrassed Lew and made his voice sharper than usual.

He said: "J.W.'s sick. He ought to be in bed. Where's Max? I want to send him to town for the doctor."

Her eyes left his face and she looked at her husband. Concern filled her eyes at once. She murmured: "Come on, John. I'll fix your bed. I knew you should have taken better care of that cough."

Lew repressed a smile. Leona changed moods as easily as she changed clothes. Right now she was the devoted, concerned wife. But an instant before, her steady glance at Lew had been deliberately wanton and inviting.

He watched her help J.W. up the stairs, and the surprising part of it was that the old man seemed to welcome the help. Lew frowned. This wasn't like him.

He sat down where Leona had sat, feeling the warmth of the cushions beneath him. Within himself, he wasn't too hard on Leona. She was thirty-five, half J.W.'s age. J.W. still had his lusty male hungers, but they didn't show themselves often, which left Leona, lusty herself, frustrated and unsatisfied most of the time.

She didn't regret her bargain in marrying J.W. Lew knew that. And her flirtations and affairs were discreet. J.W. never got wind of any of them. At least Lew didn't think he did. But it bothered Lew when Leona looked at him that way. It made him feel disloyal to J.W. because he couldn't help thinking what it would be like bedding with Leona. He didn't want her, and she embarrassed him, but all the same she stirred in him the hungers of a questing male.

He got up nervously, hearing the low, indistinct murmur of voices from the second floor. There were three bedrooms up there, and J.W.'s office, but nobody slept up there but Leona and J.W. The other rooms were reserved for guests.

He went back outside and walked along the gallery until he came to Max's room. He pushed it open without knocking.

Max sat at a table, a disassembled revolver spread out before him. He looked up in his oddly child-like way. "Some storm, wasn't it, Lew?"

"It was." Lew stared thoughtfully at Max. Max was J.W.'s third son, and had just turned twenty-one this spring. He was gigantic, the strongest man Lew had ever seen. His biceps were as big as Lew's thighs. And he had the mind of a twelve-year-old boy. His hair was like yellow silk and he seldom had it cut, so that now it curled over his neck and around his ears. His eyes were faded blue, his face as smooth and unlined as a child's. There was no meanness in Max. Except when he was drunk. Then, for some reason, he hated the world and everything in it. He wanted to fight everyone he saw, preferably all together. Joe Riker, the sheriff at Medicine Lodge, shuddered every time he saw Max come into town.

Lew said: "J.W. and I got caught in the storm. J.W.'s sick. It's that damned cough he's had, and getting chilled and all, I guess.

I think Doc ought to see him. Mind riding in for him?"

"Sure not, Lew. I'll do it now."

He got up, wiping his oily hands on a rag. Lew smiled at him. Max might not have much in the way of a mind, but he was pleasant enough and the best gunsmith Lew had ever known. He seldom did any work around .45, but he kept everybody's guns in shape, and even did gun work, gratis, for others in the county. All they had to do was ask.

Lew cautioned: "No liquor, Max."

Max giggled sheepishly. "I promise, Lew."

"Fine. And hurry. It could be lung fever."

He watched Max go out. Max walked down through the open gates and swung right toward the corral. A few moments later, Lew saw him ride past the gate again, his horse loping easily.

Lew walked along the gallery to the front door. The clouds overhead were breaking up now, and caught the dying rays of the setting sun. The hail had chilled the air, and Lew shivered slightly. There was weariness in him from the chilling, pelting hail, from the bruising, brutal fight with Roma. He raised a hand and touched his nose gingerly. Then he grinned to himself, thinking it must look like a ripe tomato.

Sobering, he stepped into the house. Leona had just come downstairs. He said: "I sent Max for Doc. How's J.W.?"

"Feverish. Weak. I wish I'd made him stay in bed with that cough. But you know him as well as I do. He's stubborn as a mule."

Lew wished suddenly that he'd gone for the doctor himself instead of sending Max. Not that he didn't trust Max. But he might have made it to town a little faster himself. He broke off his thoughts with wry disgust, knowing Max would make it just as fast as he, knowing Max would not foul it up.

Leona studied his face. "It must have been some fight."

Lew grinned at her. "It was."

"Who was it with, and what was it about?"

"I doubt if you know him. Name's Roma. He's a newcomer to the country. He was over at Santoyo's, pawing Natalia."

Leona murmured: "Galahad Stark to the rescue. Did it ever occur to you that maybe she didn't want to be rescued?"

Lew frowned angrily. "She's only seventeen."

Leona smiled tolerantly. "You don't know much about women, do you, Lew?"

"I guess not." The direction the conversation was taking made him nervous and uneasy.

"Somebody ought to teach you."

He said irritably: "For God's sake, Leona, drop it. J.W.'s sick and this isn't the time."

She flushed and for an instant her eyes sparkled angrily. Then there was contrition in her face, though her eyes still rested on him, an unsatisfied hunger in their depths.

Lew said: "I'm sorry, Leona."

"I ought to be the one who's sorry."

Lew paced back and forth across the room. He was near exhaustion, but worry and nervousness wouldn't let him rest. Sometimes, like now, he pitied Leona, though he was careful not to let it show. She was so damned twisted up inside. Basically decent, she hated herself for her wantonness, but she just couldn't seem to help it. *Maybe J.W. knew,* thought Lew suddenly. *Maybe he knew and understood. It would be like him.*

Lew went out to the kitchen and got a brown bottle of whiskey down from the shelf. He dumped out a half glassful and gulped it down.

Leona, who had followed him, watched from the doorway. "Hungry, Lew?"

He considered that before he answered. At last he nodded. "I guess I am. Maybe that's what's the matter."

"I'll fix you something." She busied herself with the stove.

63

She got a side of bacon from the porch and sliced it. She seldom did any cooking, and the fact that she was doing it now, instead of calling Rosa, betrayed her desire to be alone with Lew, to do some of the things a wife might do for him, even if she couldn't do them all.

He sat down at the table and she immediately brought him a cup of coffee. He watched her covertly as she moved around.

Leona was perhaps the most complicated person Lew had ever known. She came from the same Texas town from which J.W. had originally come. Five years ago she'd shown up suddenly in Medicine Lodge and had hired a rig to ride out to .45. She'd asked for J.W. and had talked with him over an hour up in his office. After that she'd gone back to Medicine Lodge. And in the days following, J.W. made regular trips to town to see her. A month after her arrival they were married.

To Lew, it looked as though she had come to Medicine Lodge for the specific purpose of marrying J.W., and the speed with which she'd accomplished it was a source of mild amazement to him. But J.W. had apparently never regretted his action in marrying her. She satisfied his wants and managed his house. And if she couldn't keep her eyes off his sons and every other man that came around, what matter? J.W. lost nothing. She never withheld herself from him.

Lew sometimes speculated about what had been said between them that first day in J.W.'s office. He had a vague notion it concerned him, because after he met Leona, J.W. had acquired a strange way of watching Lew. And Lew had sometimes caught him frowning to himself as though he were worried.

Leona put a sizzling platter of eggs and bacon before Lew. She brought him a plate of still-warm rolls from the warming oven above the stove. She refilled his coffee cup and then sat down across from him.

He ate hungrily, and afterward leaned back and made a

64

smoke. He grinned. "That did it. I feel as though I could sleep for a week."

"Then go to bed. I'll wake you when the doctor comes." He hesitated, his eyes half-closed. Leona said: "Lew, there's nothing you can do for him and you're beat. Now go to bed. I promise to call you the instant the doctor comes."

"That'll be about midnight."

"Yes." She avoided his eyes, flushing a little, not wanting him to see the expression her own eyes held. Lew nodded, got up, and went out the kitchen door onto the gallery. He looked back from the doorway and grinned. "Thanks for the feed."

She didn't reply, so he closed the door and walked along the now dark gallery to the door of his room. He opened it, sat down in the darkness, and removed his boots. He lay down on the bed, thinking of J.W. He was oddly apprehensive. Then sleep took him and he knew no more.

IV

When Lew awoke, the room was gray with the cold light of early dawn. He lay still for a moment, puzzled at the ache in his bones, at the fact that he was fully dressed and not even in his own clothing. Then, suddenly, memory returned. Something had happened! Leona had promised to wake him the instant the doctor came and that should have been hours ago.

Leaping off the bed, he yanked a clean shirt and a pair of his own jeans out of the closet. He put them on hastily, also clean socks and his boots, and at last belted his cartridge-studded belt and holstered gun around his hips.

He went out and hurried along the brick-paved gallery to the kitchen door. He banged inside, finding it dark and cold. On through the house he went, and upstairs to J.W.'s room.

Leona sat in a chair beside the old man's bed. Her head had fallen to one side and she was sound asleep. A lamp smoked unheeded on the ornate dresser top.

Lew looked at J.W.'s waxen face. He listened to the harsh rasp of J.W.'s breathing. He put a hand on J.W.'s flushed forehead. It was dry and incredibly hot.

He whirled and left the room, hearing a sleepy, waking sound from Leona as he did.

Where in the hell was Max? What in God's name had happened, and why wasn't the doctor here? J.W. was in damned bad shape.

He banged out of the house and ran along the gallery to the gates. As he approached the corral, he saw the cook shack window light up as the cook lit his lamp. Lew guessed it was probably 4:00 a.m.

He roped out the fastest horse in the corral, a leggy, gleaming bay, and flung his saddle to the gelding's back. Then, swinging to the saddle, he spurred away. The gelding wanted to buck the morning chill from his body, but Lew wouldn't let him. Instead, he held the bay's head up with an inflexible hand on the reins, and made the horse run.

The road was washed out a mile from the house. Lew let the bay pick his way down the arroyo's sides and up again, making a mental note to send someone out with a team and fresno to repair it as soon as he got home again. Puddles and ponds glistened in the early morning light everywhere he looked, but the road underfoot was firm. He held the horse at a steady lope until sweat darkened the bay's glossy neck and turned to foam.

The bay was wheezing harshly as Lew rode into Medicine Lodge just a little after 6:00. A sign at the edge of town claimed a population of one hundred and seventy-six. There were three streets to the town, Center in the middle, Cheyenne on the left, and Regal on the right. Doc lived on Regal, the residential street. Center held the town's business houses. Cheyenne was a street of livery barns, saloons, Lily's place, and a collection of shacks in which the town's poorer population lived. At the far end of Center was the sheriff's office, and behind it, on Cheyenne, was the jail, a stone-block building about twenty feet square.

Lew turned at the first intersection and thundered east to Regal. He swung down before the sagging picket gate that led to the doctor's weathered old two-story house.

The doctor's wife, attired in freshly starched gingham and a sunbonnet to match, was already out weeding her flower beds. She looked up, startled by Lew's apparent haste. "Somebody hurt, Lew?"

"Not hurt. Sick. It's J.W. Where's the doc?"

"Still abed, Lew. I'll call him."

She got to her feet, dusting moist earth from her hands.

Lew said: "Hurry, Missus Dawson, J.W.'s real bad, I think."

She glanced at his face, then hurried into the house. Lew heard her calling upstairs shrilly for Doc Dawson. She came back then, and stuck her head out the door. "Harness his buggy horse for him, Lew. And hitch up, will you?"

"Sure." Lew started away, then turned and called: "He can get breakfast at Forty-Five!"

He ran to the stable behind the house and harnessed Doc's gray to the buggy. He drove out, through the vacant lot, and stopped before the house.

Doc came out, jamming on his black derby, and placed his bag on the seat. Lew said quickly: "Max . . . didn't he come?"

Doc's puzzled expression told him Max had not come.

Lew said: "J.W.'s had a cough for a week. Yesterday he got caught in that storm. This morning his breathing sounds like a wind-broken horse and he's hot as the top of a stove."

Doc nodded, got in, and took up the reins. He drove his horse out of town at a lope without looking back.

Lew hesitated a moment, torn between following him and

staying in town long enough to locate Max. He wanted to know why Max hadn't sent the doctor out, and he knew he couldn't help at .45 anyway.

He swung to his saddle and rode west to Center. Seeing no one, he turned the corner and rode to Cheyenne. There were two broken windows in the Ace High. Shards of glass still littered the walk. Lew rode close and saw the brown stains of recent blood on the boards. Last night's blood, he guessed. Probably caused by Max.

He could imagine the shambles inside the Ace High. J.W. would get a bill for that. When Max went wild, he did it up brown. But why had Max failed to send the doctor out? That wasn't like him. That wasn't like him at all.

Lew swung his lathered horse and rode up to Center. He swung left there and dismounted before the sheriff's office.

It was locked. Lew hesitated between using this time to change horses at the stable and hunting up Joe Riker. He fished a sack of tobacco and papers from his pocket and made a smoke. He lit it and dragged the smoke deep into his lungs.

He turned toward his horse, and from a corner of his eye caught the shape of Joe Riker as he stepped from the verandah of Ma Jankovich's boarding house down the block. He leaned back against the building wall, waiting. Impatience tugged at him.

Joe Riker was a short, bow-legged man who walked with a rolling gait. His shoulders seemed incredibly broad and solid— probably because he was a short man—and tapered downward to his hips and thighs like a sharpened wedge. He was dressed in wool pants, well-worn tooled boots, and wore a bright plaid flannel shirt. If he saw Lew, it didn't hurry him, but in due time he reached the office, and fumbled in his pocket for his keys. He nodded shortly at Lew. "Come after Max?"

"He's in jail?"

Riker looked at him irritably. "Where else? He damned near wrecked the Ace High. J.W.'s going to have a hell of a bill to pay on this."

Lew frowned. "J.W.'s sick, Joe. I sent Max in for Doc. I can't understand. . . ."

Riker didn't reply. He unlocked his office and stepped inside. He put up the shades at the windows. Leaving the front door open, he unlocked the back door and stepped into the alley. Lew followed, irritability tugging at him. *My God, couldn't Max do even a simple thing like notifying Doc that his father was sick and needed care?* Lew remembered his trepidation about sending Max last night and wished he'd come himself. If he'd known it would turn out this way. . . .

By following a well-worn path through the weeds, they reached the door to the jail, which was in the rear. The door was built of creosoted railroad ties fastened together with heavy straps of wrought iron, and was secured by a hasp and padlock. Lew had never seen a larger padlock in his life.

Riker unlocked it, put his shoulder against it, and the door swung ponderously open. They entered the jail, which was cool to the point of being chilly.

A groan reached Lew's ears as he stepped inside. He looked across toward the two barred cells. One held Max, sitting on a cot holding his head in both hands. The other was empty.

Riker crossed to the cell door and unlocked it. He swung it open; it creaked protestingly. Riker said unsympathetically: "All right, Max. Come on."

Max dropped his hands and looked up. His eyes narrowed against the bright sunlight streaming in the open door, and he winced with the pain in his head.

His lips were puffy and bruised. There was a blue mouse about the size of a marble on one cheek bone. His left eye was blue and swollen almost shut. His knuckles were skinned and bleeding, the scabs having been broken open by the clenching and unclenching of his fists. His eyes were shamed and sheepish. He was meek as a whipped collie.

"I'm sorry, Lew. Honest, I am. I don't know what comes over me."

"I sent you for Doc." Lew's voice was hard.

Max looked up, meeting Lew's eyes for the first time. There was honest bewilderment in Max's dumb look. He rumbled: "And I sent him, Lew."

"Don't lie to me, Max. Doc didn't know anything about J.W. being sick. I just now sent him out."

"But Ira said. . . ."

"What did Ira say, Max?" Gentleness had come into Lew's tone. Gentleness and another quality, a deadly, angry one.

"He promised to send Doc out to see J.W. He said I'd had a long ride in the cold and wet . . . I *was* wet, Lew, and cold . . . and I needed a drink. He left, and when he came back, he said Doc was on his way."

Lew's body felt cold. Something kept jumping in the pit of his stomach. He looked down at his hands and saw they were clenched until the knuckles showed white.

He spoke with forced quiet. "All right, Max. You go on home."

Max looked at his face, and winced like a small boy whose father is suddenly and unexpectedly angry. Lew repeated in a gentler tone: "Go on home, Max."

He watched Max stumble out the door, then swung to face Riker. "You know who ought to be in jail for last night, don't you?"

"Ira?"

"No, not Ira, although he's to blame, too. Glen Fish. The son-of-a-bitch knows what liquor does to Max. I'm going to tell J.W. not to pay that damage claim. Maybe if Fish has to stand his own damage this time, he'll refuse to sell drinks to Max the next time."

"He'll press charges against Max."

"Let him. I'll run the bastard clear out of the country."

Riker gave him a steady look. "Don't try to run me, Lew. Don't try to run my county or any part of it."

"Then run it yourself. There's nobody in this whole damned country easier to get along with than Max when he's sober. It's up to you to see that nobody in Medicine Lodge sells him whiskey."

They exchanged stares, and Riker's glance dropped first. He grumbled: "All right, Lew. I'll tell 'im." He lifted his eyes and they showed a faint residue of anger. "But you tell Ira. He's the one that brought it up."

Lew said—"Fair enough."—and put an apologetic hand on Riker's powerful shoulder.

Riker went out, and Lew followed. Riker turned and relocked the jail. He walked across the lot and entered the back door of his office.

Lew cut away at the back door and circled the building. He mounted, rode back to Cheyenne, and along it to the livery barn, with a sour glance at the closed Ace High as he passed.

He exchanged his lathered horse for a fresh one at the stable, and then rode out again. Hesitating in the street, he felt a rush of concern about J.W. Doc must be halfway to .45 by now. He wondered how J.W. was, and wished the old man were younger. Damn it, age was treacherous. It stole your vitality and resistance to sickness.

Lew looked uptown toward Ma Jankovich's boarding house. It was a three-story structure and its ornate but shabby elegance was visible above the roofs of the surrounding buildings.

Lew wanted to see Ira. He wanted to confront Ira with his treachery in failing to send Doc out to .45 last night. But that

71

ld have to wait. Right now, J.W.'s condition was the only thing that mattered.

V

Riding south toward .45, Lew's temper smoldered like an underbrush fire when the wind has died. He wondered why Ira had failed to send the doctor. Was it pure cussedness? Or was there a deeper, more obscure motive?

Ira Regal was the old man's second son. He was twenty-two and had gone through law school up at Denver and had passed the Colorado bar. Then he'd returned to Medicine Lodge to practice. Six months later, he had taken in his shingle without having handled a single case, and had accepted employment in the office of aged Will Robinson, where he now did paperwork and handled minor matters, particularly those that required long-distance riding, which Will couldn't do. Stocky and heavily built, he had an unpleasant manner that, Lew thought, was probably indicative of his own bitterness and frustration. Ira knew, as did everyone else in the county, that Will Robinson only kept him on because it was the price of .45's legal work. Perhaps due to his education, Ira seemed to hold everyone else in contempt, even his own father and Lew. He considered himself intellectual, and far above everyone else in town.

Lew's eyes hardened. Ira was the one that had been behind the effort to get J.W. declared incompetent. Perhaps he had seen that was going to fail. Perhaps now he wanted his father dead. Lew shook his head, wondering, as he often did these days, about J.W.'s sons. Why did the sons of a good man so often turn out bad? He came to no conclusions, save one, and that caused a momentary pang of guilt within him. Perhaps J.W. had given too much to Lew, too little to his own sons, his own blood kin.

The land lay steaming under the brilliant morning sun. There was not a cloud in the sky, save for a few tall white thunderheads

72

over the dim line of mountains in the west. Later, Lew supposed, they would spread eastward across the land, bringing, perhaps, thunderstorms similar to the one that had struck yesterday.

An hour passed, and part of another. Lew pushed his horse as hard as he dared in the growing muggy heat. At about 9:00, he reached the arroyo where the road was washed out. Doc's buggy sat on the near side, its shafts empty and resting on the ground.

Lew rode down into the arroyo and up on the far side, following the tracks of Doc's buggy horse. It wasn't unusual for Doc to abandon his buggy when the going got rough and go on astride his buggy horse. But it had resulted in a loss of time. Lew wished he'd thought of that washout in time to warn the doctor. Doc could have ridden out on a saddle horse and saved a lot of precious time.

A few minutes later, Lew rode through the gate and into the yard. He saw Max's horse tied before the house, lathered and trembling. He tied his own beside it and went inside.

Max sat on one of the sofas, his head in his hands. Lew saw the crust of blood on his hair for the first time. He said: "Max, before Doc goes, let him look at your head. Did Riker give you that?"

Max looked up, grinned uncertainly and said hoarsely: "I guess so, but I likely had it coming."

"Let Doc look, anyway. How's J.W.?"

"Doc's with him. He ain't come down yet."

"Then I'll go up."

He met the doctor at the top of the stairs. "How is he, Doc?" he asked. "Is it serious?"

Doc stared at him irritably through gold-rimmed spectacles. "Serious? You're damned right it's serious. J.W.'s got pneumonia. I should've seen him last night."

Lew didn't reply. "What can I do? Anything at all?"

Doc shook his head, his face softening slightly. "Nothing anyone can do now, Lew. He'll reach the crisis in an hour or so. If he makes it through that. . . ."

"What do you mean *if*? He's got to."

"He's seventy years old, Lew."

"Can I see him?"

"I suppose so, though I doubt if you'll get much sense out of him. He's been delirious ever since I got here." He took a step toward the stairs. "Rosa's got breakfast waiting. You'd better come along and eat. Leona said she'd call if there was any change."

"In a minute, Doc. I've got to see him first."

Doc clumped heavily down the stairs. Lew turned and went into J.W.'s bedroom.

There seemed to be little change in J.W. since last night except that he looked, lying there, weaker, thinner, frailer. His breathing was still rasping, but it was fainter.

Leona looked up, her face streaked with tears. "Lew, I'm scared."

He said: "So am I." He studied her face. It was haggard and drawn. He said sympathetically: "Leona, you've been here with him all night. Go down and eat something and rest a while. I'll call you if there's any change."

She hesitated, looking back and forth from Lew's to J.W.'s face. Then she got up stiffly. "All right, Lew. I would like some coffee."

He heard her steps on the stairs. He stood staring down at J.W. He felt tears burn in his eyes, felt a choked feeling in his throat. He said softly: "I'm sorry, J.W. I should have gone for Doc myself."

J.W.'s eyes opened. He grinned faintly. His eyes, Lew saw,

were rational and without delirium. J.W. said weakly: "Sit down, Lew."

Lew murmured: "I promised to call Leona and Doc if there was any change."

J.W. shook his head weakly. "I want to talk to you."

Lew sat down gingerly on the edge of the chair. He kneaded his hands together between his knees. Damn! A man was certainly helpless in the face of sickness.

J.W. said: "No use fooling ourselves, Lew. This is bad, and I might not make it."

"You'll make it."

"I've got to, for a while. Lew, I haven't got a will. I had Robinson draw one up, and Ira was supposed to bring it out for me to sign, but he never has."

Lew said: "Will be damned. You get well. That's all that matters now."

"Not to me, Lew. I want Forty-Five to go to you. Sure I want my boys taken care of if they ever need anything, and Leona, too, but I don't want them to have the ranch. That's yours."

"But they're your own sons. It's only right. . . ."

J.W. stopped him. "Don't argue, Lew. Just listen."

Lew closed his mouth.

J.W. said: "You're the one that's been like a son to me. And you're the one I owe. I owe you a debt that I can never pay. So I want you to have Forty-Five. You go, ride for town just as damn' fast as you can go. Find Ira or Will Robinson and get that will. Bring it here for me to sign."

"All right, J.W." He hesitated. "But it doesn't seem decent, leaving you at a time like this. I don't want to leave you."

"Get that will. Kill a horse if you have to, but get it back here fast." He grimaced, met Lew's eyes briefly, and looked away. His voice was weaker when he spoke. "I tried, Lew. I tried to make up to you for what I took from you down in Texas." He looked at Lew steadily now. There was pain in his eyes, and something that looked like fear. "Lew, I saw your face yesterday when you were fighting Roma. You've got your old man's temper, and if you don't control it, you'll end up as he did. I don't want that to happen. It scares me to think it might."

Lew looked at him puzzledly.

J.W. grinned faintly. "Never mind. It's too long a story. Just remember . . . killing never solves a problem. It only complicates it. Now go on, will you, Lew? And hurry."

"Sure. If that's what you want." Lew could feel tears burning behind his eyes again and brushed at them impatiently. He leaned over and gripped J.W.'s shoulder. He said: "You'll be all right. Damn it, you've got to be all right."

"Sure I will. Now move!"

Lew got up. He went to the door and glanced back. J.W.'s eyes were closed.

He ran downstairs and into the kitchen. Leona was sitting wearily at the table, sipping coffee. Doc sat across from her, rapidly demolishing a sizeable stack of buckwheat cakes. Rosa waddled about aimlessly, her swarthy face shining with perspiration. Her eyes were red from weeping.

Lew said: "J.W.'s rational. He wants me to go to town for him. Could you go back up, Leona?"

She rose at once and, wordless, left the kitchen.

Lew hurried outside, untied his horse, mounted, and rode out the gates. He rode to the corral, taking down his rope as he did. Without dismounting, he opened the gate and rode inside. He roped a horse, then swung down, and changed his saddle to the fresh one. He bridled, then removed the rope from around the horse's neck. He went back out, closing the gate behind him.

The ranch crew was gathered before the cook shack in little groups, talking in subdued tones as though loud noises could disturb J.W. They were as worried as he was, thought Lew. They all liked and respected J.W. They couldn't help themselves. J.W. had his harsh moments, and he could be as implacable as death itself when the need arose, but he was always honest, always fair. And there was a warmth in him that he never quite succeeded in keeping hidden.

He'd been a lawman in Texas. Lew knew that much of his past and nothing more. Lew thought he must have been a very good lawman, too. But the job had probably torn him apart inside. A lawman had to be harsh and unfeeling if he didn't want to be torn apart; he saw too much cruelty and suffering and human misery.

Lew swung his horse around and dug spurs into his sides. He headed past the gates at a hard run, the horse's hoofs making a dull thunder on the ground.

At first he thought he imagined the sound, but so terrifying was it that he reined to a halt. And then he heard it again, a sound that curdled his blood and made an icy hand clamp tight around his heart. It was a woman's scream, a lost, hopeless wail that was the sound of death floating out across the vast and empty land.

VI

Leona Regal climbed the steps to J.W.'s room. She heard the kitchen door slam behind Lew as he went out to saddle a fresh horse. She was weary, and felt as though she had not closed her eyes for a week. Even the feeling of guilt was dulled by exhaustion. She regretted having fallen asleep last night. She just hadn't been able to help herself.

As she stepped into J.W.'s room, she saw that his eyes were open. He looked at her, and smiled weakly. "Hello, Leona."

She went quickly to him and, stooping, put a kiss on his dry, hot forehead. "How are you feeling?"

"I'm all right. I sent Lew to town to get that will I had Ira and Will Robinson make for me. I want to sign it before it's too late."

Leona didn't say anything. She was ashamed of the quick curiosity that ran through her mind.

J.W. said: "I want to leave Forty-Five to Lew. He'll do right by both you and the boys."

Still Leona didn't speak. Anger touched her briefly, and then was gone. J.W. was right, she supposed, about his sons, at least. If J.W. left it to them, they'd bicker and quarrel over .45 until there was nothing left. But what about her? Wasn't she entitled to a part of it? Hadn't she shared J.W.'s bed and tried to make him feel young again? Hadn't she made his last years pleasant? Why, when she thought of the nights she'd lain beside him, wanting until every nerve in her body ached, and yet she'd never made him feel his failure. Damn it, she'd been a good wife to him even if she had practically blackmailed him into marrying her.

He was looking at her, and there was affection in his eyes. "Don't tell Lew about his father. At least don't tell him I killed his father. Please, Leona."

It was a piteous request. Leona felt tears spring into her eyes. She said: "I promise. He'll never hear it from me. I swear it, J.W."

He smiled faintly. "Thank you, Leona. You've been a good wife. I've never been sorry. . . ."

His voice faded, and Leona's heart suddenly felt cold. She picked up his wrist and felt his pulse. She got up and started for the door, but J.W.'s whispered voice called her back. "Nothing Doc can do for me now. Nothing anyone can do."

She faced him, hesitating.

He whispered: "I can't last until Lew gets back. Get me a paper and pencil, Leona, quick!"

She hesitated. If she obeyed him, he'd scrawl a will leaving .45 to Lew. She could dally, claiming there was no paper and pencil to be found. Nobody would ever know. J.W. wasn't going to last another ten minutes. Shame made her face flush, made her body hot. She went across the room, found a stub of a pencil and tore a scrap of paper from the doily on the dresser top.

She took it to him, gave him an old, folded newspaper on which to write. His hands seemed to have thinned overnight. The veins were blue and the flesh seemed almost translucent.

He said: "Lift me up."

She went quickly around the bed, knowing she was being a fool, but unable to refuse him. She helped him up onto his left elbow and watched him scrawl laboriously: *July 8, 1879. I bequeath .45 Ranch to Lew Stark.* He signed it *J. W. Regal.*

He fell back, exhausted. For what seemed a long while, but was actually less than a minute, he lay with his eyes closed, panting softly.

Then he opened his eyes. There was iron in him, she thought. He was almost dead right now, but he wouldn't quit. He said: "Witness it. Date it and sign your name. Write 'witness' under your name. Hurry!"

Leona seized the paper and pencil, her hands trembling. Swiftly she wrote in an uncertain hand: *July 8, 1879. Leona Regal, witness.*

J.W. smiled and, smiling, died, his eyes open and staring at her.

Leona's hand went to her mouth. Her throat closed tight. Her body froze there on the chair. And then she screamed, and screamed again.

She heard footsteps pounding on the stairs. She became conscious of J.W.'s body, of his dead eyes resting on her. She shuddered, and got to her feet. She stumbled toward the door.

Some impulse of which she was not even aware made her stuff the doily scrap into the bodice of her dress. Then Doc and Rosa burst into the room.

Hearing that scream, Lew whirled his horse and gouged his sides with the spurs. The startled animal wheeled, and plunged through the gateway into the yard. Across the yard he went, stirring up a cloud of dust from ground that had dried on top since yesterday's storm.

He flung himself from his horse at the door and plunged inside. Fear crawled in his belly, and an empty feeling of hopelessness. J.W. was dead. He knew it.

He met Doc at the door of J.W.'s room. He was coming out, his arm around a weeping Leona. Inside the room, following them out, was Rosa, huge, shapeless, blubbering like a girl.

Lew saw the truth in Doc's face and in the hysterical faces of the women. But he couldn't believe. He plunged into the room.

A sheet had been drawn up to cover J.W.'s face. Lew pulled it gently back, his hands trembling violently.

J.W. lay in death with his eyes open but robbed of the vitality that had been theirs in life. His face was pale, but he looked, except for those open eyes, as though he might be sleeping. Gently Lew closed his eyes. Then he fell on his knees beside the bed and wept, a thing he had not done for more than twenty years.

He heard the door close behind the others, heard their steps on the stairs. And gradually he regained control. But the dead, empty feeling inside him did not go away. Dazedly he went to the door, opened it, and went out into the hall. He walked downstairs and out into the kitchen, where the others were. Max had come in, and was crying openly. The sound of his weeping was a shocking thing, and Lew crossed to him. He put a hand on Max's shoulder, but Max shrugged it off.

Leona dabbed at her eyes, went to Max, and drew his head against her. And slowly his weeping ceased. He looked up at Leona with pure worship in his eyes.

Lew went out. The sun beat warmly down, but it failed to drive the chill from his body. Doc came out a few moments later and stood beside him, his hat and bag in his hand.

Lew glanced at him. "Did you look at Max's head?" It seemed to him he had to get his mind off J.W.'s dying, and the commonplace seemed the best way to accomplish it.

Doc nodded. "Bad bump, but nothing serious. Max has got a damned hard head."

Lew nodded. His mind groped around and at last he asked: "You treat Roma last night for that cut foot?"

Doc nodded again. His voice was faintly irritable. "Who the hell else would treat him? Did you do that to him?"

"Not directly. He was trying to split me in two with an axe and I stopped the swing with a singletree. The axe handle broke and the axe head went in his foot. Will he be crippled up?"

"Probably. He needn't be, if he stays off his foot until it heals. But I doubt if he'll do it. He's a peculiar bastard. Got an obsession about success. He was out of his head while I sewed him up. Kept saying that if a man didn't make it by the time he was forty, by God, he never would. Kept saying he was forty now and, by Jupiter, he was going to make it this year. What kind of business is he in anyway?"

"Cattle. He approached me for graze. Seems he's got three thousand head on the way here from Texas and hasn't got grass for them. He's in a bind."

"You turn him down?"

Lew nodded.

"Is that what the fight was about?"

Lew shook his head. "He was pawing Natalia. I just happened along because I'd got caught in the storm without a slicker and I was hunting shelter. He's a bad one, Doc. Any man that'll try and force a seventeen-year-old girl is a son-of-a-bitch in my book."

Doc looked at him quizzically. "Wouldn't have been jealousy on your part, would it? Natalia's a pretty thing."

Lew felt himself flushing. He said: "Damn you, Doc."

Doc interrupted hastily: "Never mind. I'm sorry. I was just thinking a man could do a hell of a lot worse."

"What do you mean by that?"

Doc said testily: "Do I have to mean something besides what I say?"

Lew grinned bleakly. "You usually do."

Doc looked straight at him. "All right. Maybe I was thinking about Leona. She's trouble . . . for you and for J.W.'s sons. She's trouble for any man who has her."

Lew's jaws clenched, but he didn't reply. He didn't want to discuss Leona with Doc or anyone else. But he did know that Doc was right. Leona would add to the already explosive situation at .45. Lew didn't know much about law, but he did know that in Colorado when a man dies without a will, half his estate goes to his widow, and the other half is divided among his direct descendants. Leona would get half of .45. J.W.'s sons would each get an eighth. And Lew would get nothing.

He knew it was foolish to hope that J.W.'s sons could get along with each other, or indeed that they'd even try. Every one of them, with the possible exception of Max, would probably be after Leona and Leona's one-half share, knowing that with it he would gain control of .45. And to which of them would Leona turn? Would she turn to any one of them? Or would she bring in an outsider to complicate things more.

Lew thought of Roma. He wanted .45 graze desperately. He needed it to avoid loss of his cattle and eventual ruin. Roma would be after Leona like a stallion after a mare in heat. Suddenly the loss of J.W. was like a knife turning in Lew's heart. He wondered at the things J.W. had said before he died. Puzzling things, like telling him not to turn out like his father, and that killing never solved a problem, but only complicates it.

Doc was speaking and Lew forced his mind to listen. Doc was saying: "What'd J.W. want you to go to town for, Lew?"

"He'd made a will. He wanted me to get it so he could sign it before he died."

Doc said: "Ah-hah."

Lew scowled. The thought occurred to him at the same time it apparently had occurred to Doc. Ira worked for Will Robinson. Ira knew about the will, knew its provisions. And Ira had deliberately gotten Max drunk by saying he'd send Doc out to .45. Then he'd failed to send Doc out.

Doc said: "The will wouldn't have disinherited Ira, would it?"

Lew growled: "It left Forty-Five to me."

"And now you're out in the cold."

Lew faced him squarely. "I don't think it's decent to talk about J.W.'s estate before his body's cold. I want to set you straight on one thing though . . . Forty-Five doesn't mean money and power to me. To me, it's home. Its everything I can remember. It was J.W.'s life, and it's mine. I don't care about owning it, but I'd like to live on it. And I won't stand by and see it ruined, or split up and sold off to satisfy a bunch of quarreling heirs."

"You may not have much choice."

Lew's jaw hardened. "Maybe not. But I'm going to try. I think J.W. would expect that of me."

Doc stepped off the gallery. "I wish you luck."

Lew smiled briefly. "Thanks."

Doc Dawson said: "I'll make the arrangements for J.W.'s funeral in town if you want."

Lew nodded his agreement. Then Doc mounted his buggy horse, on which harness still hung, and rode out through the gates. Lew mounted his own horse and, leading Max's, rode out himself. He turned toward the corral and when he reached it, unsaddled both animals and turned them in. Then he walked toward the bunkhouse. He spoke in a loud, harsh voice to the crew. "J.W. is dead." The words sounded unreal as he said them. He listened to the crew's response of shock and unbelief. He said: "The road's washed out about a mile toward town. Slim, you and Jess take a fresno and team and go fix it."

He knew, from the way they looked at him, that they were already wondering to whom .45 would go. They'd find out soon enough. Doc's arrival in town would start the vultures gathering. Ira and Guy and Marion Gilbert hadn't been out to .45 in months, but they'd come now, they'd come and they'd bring trouble with them.

He turned gloomily and tramped back to the house. Already he missed J.W. terribly and he knew it would get worse. Probably J.W.'s sons and Leona would force him to leave .45. He knew how jealous J.W.'s sons were of him, how they resented him. He'd have to leave, he realized. He'd have to stand helplessly by and watch .45 come apart at the seams. He'd see the monument J.W. had built crumble and fall.

His jaw hardened. Maybe he would, but not without a fight. By God, not without a fight!

VII

On the day of the funeral, rigs began to arrive as early as 9:00. They streamed across the vast land, following two-track roads, trails, and sometimes even cutting straight across country. The road from town carried a fairly steady stream, and dust lay over it like a thin haze, marking its course across the rolling land.

At .45 there existed a sort of armed truce. Lew had not

confronted Ira with his failure to send out the doctor. He intended to, but wanted to wait until after the funeral. In the meantime he stood with Leona and the brothers, greeting the mourners, literally hundreds of J.W.'s friends.

The house overflowed with them, and the yard as well. On the shady side of the outside wall, nearly thirty men who had come alone squatted on their heels and talked, about cattle, grass, poker—about anything and everything but J.W. Regal. Yet in all their minds, Lew knew, J.W.'s death was uppermost, and he knew J.W. was sorely missed.

The day dragged for Lew. Ira and Guy and Marion Gilbert, who everyone called Gib, watched him covertly, almost gloatingly. He knew they were waiting, too, waiting until the funeral was over and the folks had all gone home. Then the showdown would come. Then Ira, or Guy, would order Lew to pack up and leave, and the others would back him up.

Whether he left or not depended on Leona, and the fact that it did rankled Lew. He hated to owe Leona anything. He had a hunch there was only one way to pay a debt to Leona.

In midafternoon, after Rosa had served an enormous dinner to everyone who wanted to eat, the crowd gathered in the huge enclosure before the house and J.W.'s sons carried his casket out onto the gallery, where it rested in the shade, surrounded by banks of flowers that had been gathered and brought by those in attendance.

John Jennings, the town's Presbyterian minister, recited a prayer. He spoke then, in a sonorous voice that carried to every corner of the courtyard, of J.W.'s virtues, of his rôle as empire builder in the burgeoning new Territory of Colorado. Lew listened patiently, thinking of J.W., remembering the little things. Like a sixth birthday, when the land was new and there were no stores. Lew still had the Cheyenne war bow and quiver of arrows J.W. had given him that year. And he remembered the spotted pony J.W. had traded for with a hunting party of Arapahoes, though the pony was long since dead. He remembered a Christmas tree, a small cedar, decorated with bright scraps of red cloth torn from a suit of J.W.'s red flannel underwear, remembered J.W. singing carols in a cracked and reedy voice. He remembered other things, too. A brush with Comanches at the spring now called Comanche Springs. A long trail that he and J.W. had taken after horse thieves when he was seven. J.W. had taken him along because there was no one with whom to leave him.

Glancing out over the heads of the crowd, Lew saw Natalia Santoyo standing on tiptoe so that she could see him. There were tears in her eyes, brimming over and running down her smooth cheeks.

Then the service was over, and the casket was lifted into the back of the waiting hearse. Some of the crowd went home, but the majority followed the hearse solemnly out to the burial ground on the hill, where J.W.'s first wife lay, where a grave had been dug beside hers for J.W. himself.

Lew waited, when it was over, watching the crowd file down the hill. He heard the sounds of shovels in the damp, rocky earth as members of .45's crew filled in the grave.

All through the service he had been conscious of the appraising looks he was getting from members of the crowd. They knew that next to J.W., Lew *was* .45. They knew as well that J.W. had never signed his will, and that in its absence .45 would go to his widow and his sons. Some of them would try to grab a bite of .45 range if Lew left. Some of the bolder ones might grab some steers. But if Lew stayed, they'd keep their hands off.

Mike Santoyo and Natalia came over and stood silently beside him, one on each side. Natalia laid a small hand on his arm. Mike asked quietly: "What will you do, Lew?"

Lew shrugged. "I expect that'll be decided for me. I have no rights here, Mike."

"You reckon that's the way J.W. would want it?"

Lew shook his head. "No, but that's the way it is."

"Not unless you let it be."

Lew looked at Mike's leathery face. Mike said: "I got my walking papers a while ago."

Anger stirred in Lew. "Who from?"

"Ira. Guy backed him up. Said there'd be no damn' squatters on Forty-Five from here on."

Lew felt his face flush with growing anger. "You're no squatter. You were here when J.W. got here."

Mike shrugged.

Lew asked incredulously: "You're not going, are you?"

"No, not unless I go in a box."

Lew felt Natalia's hand tighten on his arm. He covered it with his own and found it cold.

He said: "Mike, take Natalia home. I don't want either you or her to see this. It won't be nice."

Mike studied his face. Then, without a word, he turned and stalked away, walking proudly and easily, like an Indian chief. Natalia stood on tiptoe and placed a light kiss on Lew's mouth. She whispered—"Good luck, Lew."—then turned and followed Mike.

Lew felt a warmth he hadn't felt before. His eyes stayed on Natalia's slim, straight form until she passed out of sight within the gate. Still he lingered and saw them ride out a bit later. Then, satisfied that they were the last, that everyone else had gone, he made his way down the hill and entered the gate in the adobe wall.

The sun was just dropping behind the western mountains. Thunderheads in the east caught its dying glow and put an orange light over all the land.

Lew saw the brothers, Ira, Guy, Max, as well as Gib, standing together before the door. Guy's lips moved as Lew came in the gate.

He smiled inwardly. They were wary of him, and that was good. But there was determination in them, too, and this was the showdown, four against one.

No one else was in sight, though Lew suspected that Leona was somewhere watching, listening. For a brief instant, he felt like an outcast. He was about to be evicted from the place that had been his home, from the place he had settled and helped to build. He was being evicted because of a tie of blood and one of marriage, which the law recognized as stronger than the tie between J.W. and himself.

Crossing the yard, he studied the four brothers. Max stood on the right, hulking, his yellow mop of uncut hair still showing evidences of the slicking it had had with water just before the funeral. Max was embarrassed, and stubbornly refused to meet Lew's eyes.

Lew had a brief moment of sympathy for him. Max was in a squeeze. He had to take his stand with his brothers for loyalty's sake, but he liked Lew and didn't feel right about it. Max could be dangerous, Lew decided, if he ever got his simple mind lined out on a single course. But that wasn't likely.

Ira, squat and stocky, stood next to Max. He was scowling contemptuously, and there was a gleam of wicked anticipation in his eyes. Dislike that amounted almost to hatred stirred in Lew. If it weren't for Ira's treachery, J.W. might still be alive. And yet, in honesty, he had to admit that wasn't likely, either. There wouldn't have been much Doc could have done even if he had been called in sooner.

Guy stood next to Ira. Guy was J.W.'s eldest and perhaps had always resented Lew more bitterly than the rest, for he felt Lew had usurped the place that should rightfully have belonged to him. Guy was tall and slim, about of a size with Lew. His face was sour and almost invariably either scowling or sullen. Guy was a man with a perpetual grievance. Lew felt he was capable of anything, for he'd always be able to justify his own treachery with his ever-present grievance.

The last of the four was Gib, standing on the left. There was wildness in Gib, a recklessness that seemed to be forever getting him into trouble with the law. The companions Gib sought were the drifters, the gamblers, the women who worked Lily's place in town. They were the ones who got Gib into trouble. But Gib couldn't see it that way. Not a week before, Lew had heard him begging J.W. to give him $1,000 so he could go some place else and get a new start. Gib claimed it was a disadvantage to be related to the most powerful family in the county. Lew suspected the truth of the matter was that Gib could never, would never measure up to J.W. He knew it and he brooded on it until it warped his whole outlook on life.

There was a common quality in the faces of all four. They were like wolves, determined to pull down a full-grown bear, knowing they would necessarily suffer in the process, but not faltering in their determination.

Lew looked straight at Ira. "You! Somebody ought to kick your teeth out for the stunt you pulled the other night. You wanted J.W. to die, didn't you? You wanted him to die before he could sign his will."

Ira sneered. "Hurts, doesn't it? Here we are, all J.W.'s heirs. And Lew Stark, the favorite, is out in the cold. How's it feel?"

Lew felt the muscles in his forearm twitch. He glanced at Max, but Max was studying the ground at his feet. He switched his glance to Guy, and was surprised to see in Guy's eyes a look of murderous hatred. He said contemptuously: "What have you got to say?"

Guy held his glance, though apparently with some difficulty. Guy said harshly with tight fury: "Get off Forty-Five, you son-of-a-bitch! Pack your gear and be out of here by dark. You don't own a horse or a blade of grass."

Lew clenched his fists. He said evenly: "I'll leave when I'm ready to leave. You four represent just half of Forty-Five. I'll hear from the other half before I go."

Ira sneered. Lew wanted to smash his sneering lips against his teeth. Ira said: "Figuring to bed with the other half?"

Lew felt his knees trembling. He held onto himself with difficulty. For a long while he stared at them steadily, his eyes daring one of them to open his mouth. Then he said scathingly: "Did any of you ever ride with your father? Did any of you ever give a damn what happened to Forty-Five, as long as it supported you? Did any of you ever work at ranching it?" He snorted savagely. "There isn't a damned one of you who knows where its boundaries are, or how many cattle it ships in a year."

Max looked up, shamefaced as a twelve-year-old. "I fix all the guns around Forty-Five, Lew. You can't say I don't do nothing."

His three brothers swung their heads to glare at him with angry contempt, but Lew's face softened. "You're the exception, Max. At least you've lived on Forty-Five." Pity stirred him. Max was big enough, powerful enough to wrestle a bear and win. He could break Lew in two without even exerting himself. A pity his mind couldn't have developed like the rest of him.

Lew switched his glance to the others as Guy said: "You're leaving, Lew. Now. Right now."

Lew's face was white. "You going to make me, Guy?"

Guy chuckled. "What I'm going to say will make you leave. You'll never want to see Forty-Five again or think of J.W. Regal."

Lew looked levelly at him. "Go on."

Guy's face was white, his eyes pinched. He blurted: "J.W. shot and killed your old man down in Texas. Did you know that?"

Lew didn't reply. An icy hand closed over his heart.

Guy gained confidence from his silence. "But you ought to know why, Lew. Sure, maybe your old man *was* a killer. And J.W. was sheriff. But he didn't have to *kill* your old man. He could have taken him alive. Reason he didn't was that he wanted your ma. He'd been messin' around with her and wanted her for keeps. Only he couldn't have her as long as your pa was alive. He. . . ."

Lew's clenched, bony fist smashed against his mouth with all the drive of Lew's body behind it. Guy went back, slammed against the rough adobe wall of the house, and slid down it to the brick-paved gallery floor. Blood ran from both corners of his mouth. He spat, and two teeth came out with the bloody spittle.

Lew stood over him. Wildness had taken him, a kind of unthinking insanity that wanted only one thing—to smash, to destroy.

Guy looked up, eyes gleaming. He said: "Get him." His voice rose until it was nearly a scream. "Don't stand there! Get him!"

Lew swung around. Ira came at him from one side, Gib from the other. Max stood stupidly immobile, trying to decide to which side his loyalty belonged. Lew knew that if Max ever got into this on the side of his brothers, he'd die right here on the gallery of .45. And Max would hang for his murder. His brothers would see to that.

Lew side-stepped Ira's rush and elbowed Ira in the throat as he went past. Ira piled into Gib, and the pair turned angrily to face Lew again. Lew backed, wanting the wall of the house behind him, but Guy's foot went out, tripped him, and sent him crashing to the paving.

Ira and Gib rushed. Lew, on his back, raised both feet. They caught Gib in the belly, lifted him, and flung him back. Ira kicked out savagely, and the kick landed in Lew's ribs. Wind drove out of him in a gusty explosion. Pain lanced through his mid-section. He gagged for breath, rolling to protect his exposed belly and groin.

Guy was up now, and kicked Lew in the side of the head. It fuzzed Lew's mind, but his fury was too awesome for him to stay down long. He came up, driving forward on hands and knees. His head rang and he still gasped helplessly for breath. His head struck Ira in the thigh and tumbled his legs from under him. Lew stumbled over him and fell sprawling.

He rolled, knowing suddenly that this was the worst he had ever faced, knowing they would kick and beat him until he was dead or dying on the ground. Gib's boot swung at his head, missed, and the cartwheel spur roweled a long cut in Lew's cheek. Blood flowed from it freely, soaking his neck, dripping from his chin.

He lunged away and, a dozen feet from the edge of the gallery, stumbled to his feet. Head lowered, like a wounded bear, he waited for them to rush. They did, Gib and Ira coming from the front, Guy circling around behind.

Lew knew suddenly he couldn't fight them all and come out alive. He must pick one and concentrate on him with an eye to putting him out of the fight. While he was doing it, he'd have to absorb the punishment of the others. He'd have to absorb it and stay on his feet. He picked Gib, the wild one, the one most likely to use a gun. He turned toward Gib and sent a long, hard right smashing into Gib's face.

Ira clubbed him with both fists on the neck. Pain shot through his head and back like a knife. But he followed Gib, looping a left into Gib's mid-section, elbowing him on the ear as Gib involuntarily doubled against the pain. Gib went down, and Lew kicked him savagely in the face. He swung to meet the others, legs spread, in time to catch a wild kick that struck his thigh and slid upward to catch him in the groin.

Pain more excruciating than any he had ever felt before tore raggedly through his belly. Dimly he heard Ira's gloating voice: "God damn you, bed with the other half now. You won't be very persuasive."

Lew was sick, in pain so terrible he couldn't even straighten up. But the fury in his brain could admit no defeat. It would drive him until the blood stopped pumping from his heart. He rushed at Ira, and his hands closed like talons around Ira's throat. Back they went, to fall on the ground, struggling, kicking, blindly rolling in the choking dust. Lew's fingers dug into Ira's throat, compressing his windpipe, bruising, nearly breaking his neck. Lew's strength was the strength of a maniac, and after a furious but brief struggle Ira was still. Guy rained blows on his back and shoulders. Occasionally one struck his head. But his hands never slackened their grip.

Gib lay retching on the ground. Max, his face showing confusion and bewilderment, moved in. He rumbled—"Lew, let go."—but Lew never heard him. Max cuffed Lew, open-handed, on the side of the head.

Lew rolled for a dozen feet, his hands torn from Ira's throat. Ira lay still, as if dead, but his chest began to rise and fall.

Lew got up and rushed at Max. His fist landed squarely on Max's jaw and barely rocked his head. But it angered the dull, undeveloped mind. Max's eyes glittered. His thick lips moved. "You hadn't ought to've done that, Lew."

Lew swung again and nearly broke his hand on Max's skull. Max picked him up like a dog and flung him against the wall of the house. He struck it with a thud, then dropped soddenly to the brick paving. He was nearly out. He could see light and he could hear sound, but he couldn't move. Guy ran across the gallery and stood by Lew, looking down. Then he began to kick, methodically, viciously, his eyes gleaming, his lips drawn back from his smashed and bleeding mouth.

Suddenly, a roaring sound filled Lew's ears, followed by a

sound like hail ripping through a tree. He heard a voice, but the voice went on for several long moments before he began to distinguish the words: ". . . touch him again, and I'll blow a hole through you big enough to throw the gun through." A woman's voice. Leona's voice. Lew groaned. He turned his head and saw her blurred before his eyes. She held J.W.'s double-barreled ten-gauge in trembling hands. Its muzzle pointed straight at Guy. Her finger was curled tightly around the trigger. The hammer was back, on full cock.

Guy backed slowly, fearfully, knowing how little pressure it would take to send the charge tearing through him. His face was gray.

Max was frozen, worshipful admiration in his eyes as he stared at Leona.

Lew rolled and tried to come to his hands and knees. His body was like lead. He made it halfway, then crashed back again to the gallery floor. Unconsciousness came down across his mind like a black curtain of heavy velvet.

VIII

He could not have been out more than a few minutes. When hazy consciousness returned, he felt Leona's soft hands on his face and the cool wetness of a cloth, as she sponged dirt and blood from it. It was almost dark in the courtyard. Overhead, in the coal-gray sky, two or three stars winked.

Lew struggled to a sitting position. His body was one great, throbbing ache. His head reeled and pounded with fierce intensity. Leona said with soft savagery: "Damn them. Damn them, they'd have killed you."

Lew grinned wryly, and the contortion of facial muscles was painful.

She said: "Can you make it to your room if I help you?"

"I think so. Provided nothing's broken."

He put one hand against the adobe wall of the house, the other on Leona's shoulder. It was soft, but full and firm. He grunted as he rose, and winced with pain in his right leg.

He swayed, and leaned against the wall. Leona rose beside him, making a soft, womanly sound of sympathy. Lew chuckled. "They did a job on me."

"You didn't do so bad yourself. If it hadn't been for Max, you'd have whipped the three of them."

Lew looked around. "Where are they now?"

"Up in J.W.'s office. Probably figuring out how to get rid of you."

"It shouldn't be too hard. I've got no rights here."

"That isn't true!"

Lew glanced at her, but was unable to see her face in the almost nonexistent light. He wondered briefly at her vehemence.

She went on in a calmer tone, explaining: "This is your home. You helped build it into what it is. Without you, it would fall apart in a year."

"Then it'll have to fall apart. Because I won't be here. There's no use fighting them. They can have me evicted, or thrown in jail."

He moved away, toward his room down the gallery. He stumbled on the wash pan full of water that Leona had used to sponge his face, and almost fell. Leona caught his arm. She said fiercely: "They cannot! You're forgetting something, Lew. Half of Forty-Five is mine. And I want you here. If you leave, my half of Forty-Five won't be worth a thing."

Lew didn't reply but for an instant a warm feeling of gratitude spread through him. Then doubt dispelled it. Already he owed Leona a great deal. But for her, he'd be lying here dead on the gallery floor. Now, if he stayed, he would owe her more. And he knew what coin Leona would expect in payment. For an instant he let his mind dwell on that, and felt a stir of desire run through him in spite of his hurts. A man could do worse. Leona would never disappoint him. And probably, if she had a young man, she would quit looking around at other men. Or would she? Was it because J.W. had been old that she was like she was, or would she be that way no matter to whom she was married?

Leaning heavily on her, Lew hobbled toward his room. He felt unworthy and disloyal for an instant. J.W. was scarcely cold in his grave and already Lew was thinking of bedding with his widow. And yet, within him, he knew he was not disloyal. He was a man, not a saint, and Leona had the power to stir such thoughts in any man. J.W., if he knew, would probably grin wryly and tolerantly, and then begin to talk of something else.

Lew suspected that J.W.'s love for Leona had not been of the violent and possessive variety. J.W. hadn't been blind to the qualities in those around him. He'd known his sons for what they were and undoubtedly had known Leona for what she was, too, a human being with compelling weaknesses but with many virtues as well. J.W., Lew remembered, had been pretty much inclined to take people as they were, uncritical of their weaknesses, and perhaps this quality in him had encouraged the meanness in his sons.

Reaching his room, he pushed open the door. He hobbled inside without help from Leona, and she followed him in. Lew crossed the room, found the lamp and a match, and lit it. He trimmed the wick and turned.

Leona said compassionately: "You look awful."

Lew crossed to the mirror on the wall and peered at himself. One of his eyes was puffy. His mouth was smashed, and bleeding in two places. His face was a mass of abrasions from rolling around on the ground. Gib's spur rowel had cut deeply into his cheek.

He got a bandanna from the dresser drawer and dabbed at his bleeding mouth. Then, stooping, he found a bottle of whiskey in the bottom drawer and pulled the cork. He put it to his mouth and gulped the fiery stuff, wincing afterward at the pain it caused in his cut lips.

He set it down on the dresser. Leona crossed to it, picked it up, and took a drink herself. Suddenly Ira's sneering words were in Lew's ears: *Figuring to bed with the other half?* Lew felt his face grow warm. Obviously Leona was figuring on it.

Lew said: "I'm beat. Do you mind?"

It was Leona's turn to flush. She didn't reply, and she didn't leave. She crossed the room and sat down on the edge of the bed. Lew eyed the closed door. Irritability began to stir in him. Damn it, maybe witnessing the fight had excited Leona, but participating in it sure as hell hadn't excited him. The way he felt, a woman was the least of his desires.

Leona asked without looking up: "What do you think of me, Lew? Honestly?"

He grunted. "That's a hell of a question."

She glanced up and met his eyes almost timidly. "No, I mean it. I want to know."

He felt his irritability increase. This was neither the time nor the place to evaluate Leona. Besides, he didn't like this much frankness between them. And yet, looking at her, he suddenly pitied her. He said: "You flog yourself too god-damned much. You're a human being, just like the rest of us." He picked up the bottle and took another drink. It burned all the way down.

She said, smiling faintly: "I thought that you, of all people, would at least be honest with me, Lew."

The whiskey felt warm in his stomach. "What do you want me to say? That you're a floosie? I don't think you are, though, by God, sometimes you act like one. Hell, J.W. couldn't have been much of a husband for a woman like you. There was bound to be more in you than there was in him. But why beat yourself over the head because there was? You never hurt him. You never held back from him. You did your part. What the hell else were you supposed to do?"

There were tears in her eyes. Lew said: "Damned if I know any perfect people. I don't think I'd even want to." He looked straight into her eyes and said something he wouldn't have said except for the whiskey he'd consumed. "There're times when I want you, but tonight isn't one of them. Now go on, get out of here, and let me go to bed."

Leona got up from the edge of the bed. She crossed to him and put her hands gently on the sides of his face. Standing on tiptoe, she kissed him lightly on the lips. "Thank you, Lew."

Suddenly, then, her face contorted. She whirled and ran across the room. She burst out of the door onto the gallery, leaving the door open behind her. He heard her running steps receding on the brick-paved gallery floor, until they were almost gone. An instant later he heard the heavy house door slam.

He frowned with exasperation. Damned if he knew how to figure women. He wondered if a man ever did. But the effort of thinking was too much. Exhaustion suddenly overcame him. His body ached and his head throbbed.

He bent to remove his boots and almost fell. He stumbled to the side of the bed and, raising his feet one by one, took off his boots, successfully this time. He stood up and took off his torn coat, his shirt and tie, and pants.

Then, without even looking at the damage to his body, he blew out the lamp, crossed the room, and fell limply on the bed. He was almost instantly asleep.

Leona was crying openly as she came into the big main house. She was angry, too, angry at herself and that was, perhaps, the reason she wept. She admitted to herself that the fight had stirred her. It had made her want Lew with an overpowering intensity that she had barely been able to control. She hated him briefly because he had not been observant enough to notice this, and then, realizing she was being unreasonable, crossed the room and sat down heavily on one of the rawhide-strung sofas.

Unsatisfied desire throbbed in her. She thought briefly of the brothers upstairs, and hated herself because she did. God! Didn't she have any principles? She dabbed at her eyes, and forcibly switched her thoughts back to Lew. She remembered the scrap of dresser doily upon which J.W. had written his will. She wondered briefly if it would be considered a legal will. She supposed it would. She was a witness to it and could testify that J.W. had been in full possession of his faculties. Besides, the will he'd had Robinson draw would bear out his intent that Lew should have the ranch.

She hadn't mentioned it to anybody, and didn't quite know why. Perhaps she was no better than J.W.'s sons. Perhaps she was just as greedy as they, just as willing to see Lew kicked out into the cold. She had another thought and hated herself even more bitterly, because she realized suddenly that she was keeping the will for a still more devious reason. She hoped, by dangling her own interest in .45 before him, to persuade Lew to marry her. And deep inside her she believed that if Lew realized he owned all of .45 he never would. Perhaps he wouldn't anyway. Angrily she got up and began to pace back and forth across the room. Her small hands clenched until the nails bit into her soft palms.

She looked down at her body, encased in a black, snug-fitting mourning dress. Unconsciously she drew a deep breath, watching the way her breasts swelled. Damn him, what did he want? There was only five years' difference in their ages. To look at them together you'd think there was none at all. There was no gray in Leona's hair, no lines in her face.

She heard steps on the stairs and started violently. She swung around and saw the four brothers descending. Guy was in the front.

Guy scowled at her, but in Ira's face there was frank appraisal. She could almost read Ira's mind. He was thinking that Leona's share, combined with his own, would give him control of .45. He was removing her clothes in his mind, taking her, and deciding marriage to her would not be too unpalatable, in spite of the difference in their ages, on the day of his father's funeral. Sudden anger made Leona's eyes sparkle. She knew suddenly that if she did marry Ira, that sharp, scheming mind of his would not be satisfied until he could get her interest in .45 away from her. Then he'd abandon her without mercy.

She said coldly: "There seems to be one little detail the four of you have overlooked. As J.W.'s widow, I inherit half of Forty-Five. And since I doubt if the four of you can ever agree on anything, that will give me control."

None of them spoke. With the exception of Max, they just hated her with their eyes. In Ira's eyes was contempt, which only fanned Leona's anger.

She went on tightly: "Lew is staying at Forty-Five as foreman, whether you like it or not."

Guy opened his mouth to speak, his face white with rage, but Ira put a restraining hand on his arm. "Wait, Guy. Wait. I'll figure a way."

Leona said contemptuously: "Yes. You'll figure a way, and Guy will, and Gib will, too. But the way you figure won't include the others, will it?"

They glanced at each other suspiciously. Max looked on dumbly, not comprehending the undercurrents among them. Leona said suddenly: "Max, you wouldn't want to see Lew kicked out, would you? You know he's always been good to you. You know J.W. wanted him to stay."

Max glanced at his brothers uneasily. He mumbled: "Well, I

don't know. . . ."

Leona said softly: "You'd better know soon, Max. Because I'll tell you what is going to happen. Between Lew and myself, we're going to kick the bunch of you out. How would you like to leave Forty-Five, Max?"

The stricken look on his face made her ashamed. Max rumbled quickly: "No! Don't send me away. Please, Leona. I wouldn't know what I'd do away from Forty-Five."

"Then how about Lew, Max?" Guy tried to break in, but Leona's implacable voice overrode him. "How about Lew, Max?"

Max said: "He can be foreman. That's all right with me." He looked apologetically at his brothers. "Lew's been runnin' Forty-Five. He's the only one of us who knows how."

Ira's eyes had become speculative again. Guy was in a towering rage. Gib seemed to be preoccupied, as though he had something else on his mind.

Leona said harshly: "Now go on back to town, the three of you. There's nothing for you here. Will Robinson can distribute the year's profits after we ship in the fall. Until then, I'd just as soon not see your greedy, ugly faces."

Guy glowered at her, but he turned and headed for the door. Ira smiled faintly, confidently, as though he were sure Leona would come around in time. Gib still seemed preoccupied.

Max stood, shifting his great, ponderous weight from one foot to the other. When his brothers left, he looked at Leona fearfully. "You reckon Lew will be mad at me for what I done to him? I . . . I. . . ."

Leona interrupted gently: "I don't think so, Max. Now go to bed and get some sleep."

He nodded, and shuffled uncertainly from the room.

IX

Alameda Roma had been in bed now for three days with his injured foot. It was a mass of heavy bandages, and in spite of the morphine the doctor gave him three times every day, it throbbed and pained with merciless intensity. Pain from his other injuries had subsided somewhat. But his burning hatred for the man who had done this to him had not dimmed. Indeed, it seemed to increase with every hour that passed.

His mind had not even touched on the possibility that his troubles were his own fault. He had not considered that if he had not tried to kill Lew with the axe, its head could not have gone into his foot. He was a big man, with broad shoulders and a thick, muscular barrel chest. His hips and thighs, encased in long underwear, were narrow almost to the point of appearing spindly for the weight they must support.

He got out of bed impatiently and hobbled over to his window, walking awkwardly on the crutches Doc had provided for him. He stared angrily into the street. Damn it, this had set him back, and he couldn't afford to be set back. He had three thousand cattle on the way here from Texas. As nearly as he could guess, they'd arrive within two weeks.

Before they arrived, he had to have range or else he'd have to sell the cattle and take a loss. His own resources would be wiped out. Wiped out at forty. Without a dime. In no better shape than he'd been when he'd run away from Fort Alameda twenty-eight years ago. And all because of a damned Mexican wench. All because of a quixotic fool who was willing to kill a man to protect her virtue.

Roma spat angrily out the window. If Lew Stark had stayed out of it, she'd have come around. These damned Mexican women just want to make a man fight for it a little. Still, it had been a stupid business. Now, Lew Stark, who ran .45, wouldn't lease him range even if he was willing to pay a dollar an acre.

Stark wouldn't lease at any price. If only that damned rain hadn't driven him to Santoyo's for shelter, he might have changed Stark's mind.

Roma's brain seethed. His heavy, stubborn jaw clenched. He wasn't going to be cheated of his chance. He wasn't! There had to be a way! He knew J.W. was dead. Doc had told him that. Suddenly an idea occurred to him. He didn't know who would inherit .45, but while it was tied up in an estate, he just might be able to lease in spite of Lew Stark. He might be able to lease from the estate.

He turned suddenly. He threw one of the crutches viciously against the wall. Then, hobbling on the other, he crossed the room to the closet. He flung his clothes across the room onto the bed. Crossing to them, he sat down and began to dress.

The pants barely went over the bandaged foot. He slipped on a shirt and put a boot on his unhurt foot. He rubbed a hand over his unshaven jaw, then scowled and ran his fingers through his hair. He'd hit the barbershop first. It was only good sense to be halfway presentable when he appeared to ask for the lease. He hobbled down the stairs, growing angrier with each difficult step.

The clerk at the desk stared at him, then hurried across the lobby. "You shouldn't be walking on that foot, Mister Roma. Doc said. . . ."

"To hell with Doc," Roma said savagely.

The clerk was silent. He watched Roma hobble out the door to the street and turn toward the barbershop next door. Roma fumed impatiently while the barber shaved him and cut his hair. He supposed Will Robinson would be handling the estate, since he was the only lawyer in town. So, when the barber had finished, he made his difficult way diagonally across the street to Robinson's office over the Medicine Lodge Bank.

By the time he reached the top of the stairs, he was panting

Lewis B. Patten

heavily and his body was bathed with sweat. The foot pained
him excruciatingly. He'd have cheerfully killed Lew Stark if he
could have seen him then. Instead, he stood leaning against the
wall at the top of the stairs, willing his anger to go, knowing he
would not get what he wanted from Robinson if he went in
there in this frame of mind.

Then, his face composed, he walked unsteadily along the hall
until he came to Robinson's office. He opened the door and
went inside.

Robinson must have been eighty-five, Roma guessed. He was
a tall, very thin man whose bony frame testified that he had
once been a bigger man than Roma himself. Robinson's face
was craggy and deeply seamed. His eyes were gray and tired,
but there was sharpness in them still, and wisdom, and vast
patience.

Roma looked at him and made a spare smile. "You handling
the Regal estate?"

Robinson nodded.

Roma made the smile grow wider. He stuck out a hand. "I'm
Alameda Roma. I've got cattle coming here from Texas and
need graze for them. I'll pay the going price . . . or better . . .
but I need a commitment on it right away."

"Have you seen Lew Stark?"

Roma eyed him suspiciously. Surely Robinson had heard of
the fracas he'd had with Lew Stark. He said: "You know I have.
That's how I got this foot."

"Lew turn you down?"

Roma nodded. "Even before the fight."

"Why?"

"Stubbornness or personal reasons. How do I know? The
point is that it's to Forty-Five's advantage to lease that grass.
They're not using it. They haven't enough cattle to cream more
than the top off their range. And they could use the money. I'd

pay fifteen cents a head for the balance of the summer. That'd be damn' near five hundred dollars. It'd be like finding it in the street."

Robinson shook his head. "Lew's running Forty-Five. I just handle the legal matters connected with the estate. See him again. If he'll lease, it's all right with me."

Roma scowled. For a few moments he glowered at Robinson, then turned and banged out the door.

In the hall he stopped, his mind busy. There had to be a way to get this done. He saw a man climbing the stairs and recognized Ira Regal. When Ira reached the top of the stairs, Roma said: "Aren't you one of the Regals?"

Ira nodded.

"Could I talk to you?"

"Sure. Come on in the office."

Roma shook his head. "No. This is personal. I'd as soon nobody heard."

Ira looked puzzled.

Roma said: "I'll buy you a drink."

He started to hobble toward the stairs, and Ira noticed his foot apparently for the first time. "Aren't you the one who tangled with Lew?"

"That's right."

It seemed to settle Ira's doubts, and Roma smiled inwardly. Here was a man as anxious as he was to get Lew Stark. Here was a man with whom he might do business.

Ira followed him slowly down the stairs. At the bottom, he held the outside door so that Roma could go through.

Together, then, they moved along the street, turned the corner, and headed for the Ace High. Ira found a table in the cool shadows at the rear, and waited while Roma sat down heavily.

Roma was sweating again and pain ran all the way to his

thigh. He said: "I need to lease some range. Lew Stark refused to lease Forty-Five, so I thought I'd come to you."

"I don't have the authority to lease."

"I know you don't. But you could lease to me anyway. Maybe it wouldn't be legal, but it would be legal enough to stop Stark from forcibly evicting me, wouldn't it?"

Ira frowned doubtfully. "It might."

"Then how about it?"

Ira shook his head, rising. "No. There's nothing in it for me but a few hundred dollars and a lot of grief." He must have seen the way Roma's expression darkened. He hesitated a moment, then said: "I won't do it, but I can tell you who to go to."

"Who?"

Ira began to smile. "My brother Gib. He wants to leave the country and he needs money to do it, money he can't get from the estate. He wouldn't give a damn how much trouble he left behind. He wouldn't care if you killed Lew Stark."

"Where'll I find him?"

Ira smiled. "You won't have to go far. That's him over at the bar. Want me to call him over?"

Roma nodded. Ira got up and strolled to the bar and Roma watched with interest. Ira stopped behind a tall, young, good-looking man of about twenty. Gib Regal had a narrow, somewhat vacant face and dark, brooding eyes. His mouth had a sullen, dissatisfied look to it. Roma smiled faintly. *This one shouldn't be hard to deal with,* he thought.

Ira spoke to Gib for several moments in a low voice. Gib turned, frowning slightly, and stared at Roma. Then the pair of them crossed to where Roma sat.

Ira said: "Gib, this is Alameda Roma. He's offering to lease Forty-Five range for some cattle he has coming here from Texas." Ira smiled enigmatically. "Good luck, Mister Roma."

"Thanks." Roma watched Ira turn and leave the saloon. Then

he looked at Gib. "Sit down, won't you?" He smiled pleasantly.

Gib pulled out a chair and straddled it, resting his arms on its back.

Roma said: "Your brother said you might be interested in giving me a lease."

Gib didn't answer. He looked at Roma and then away, but not before Roma had seen the cupidity in his eyes. Roma's smile widened. "I'd be willing to pay five hundred dollars to lease for the remainder of the year."

"How many cattle?"

"Three thousand head."

"The lease wouldn't be any good. You know that, don't you?"

"Legally I don't suppose it would. The thing is, it would have to be challenged in court. That would take time, and all I need is time."

He could almost see Gib's mind working behind his greedy eyes. Gib said: "Five hundred isn't very damn' much money. Not enough for a man to leave the country and make a fresh start some place else." He seemed to hesitate. "No. I guess not. I can wait until after the cattle are shipped in the fall. I'll get my cut of the profits then."

Roma said: "You want more money?" Anger stirred in him, and contempt for Gib Regal.

"Well, that ain't it altogether. I. . . ."

"What if I give you more money?"

"How much?" Gib's face with sweating slightly now. He kept licking his lips and his gaze would not meet Roma's steadily.

"Depends. Maybe if you'd give me a year's lease, I'd be willing to double the price."

"A thousand?"

Roma nodded. His eyes held a warning expression. "But don't think you can jack it up any higher. You can't."

Gib's hands clenched and unclenched in front of him. He

shifted uneasily in the chair. He said: "Cash?"

"Cash." Roma smiled faintly. "You can have it today. You can be a thousand miles from here before Lew Stark finds out I've got a lease." He tried to keep the contempt he was feeling out of his face. Here was a man born to wealth and position, with a heritage that Roma himself would give his life for, and willing to sell it out to a stranger.

Suddenly Gib nodded. "All right. I'll do it." He seemed relaxed now, almost limp. And scared.

Roma said: "All right. Go get your brother to make out the papers. Bring them back here."

"You got the money on you?"

Roma nodded. Gib stared at him a moment, then got up and hurriedly left the saloon.

Roma's face twisted unpleasantly. He thought of his own childhood at Fort Alameda, Arizona, the brawling, the fighting, the contempt shown him because of the fact that his mother did washing and whored on the side. He remembered staring into the officers' quarters sometimes, seeing them and their fine ladies eating and drinking and laughing, remembered swearing that someday he would be like them. No. He would not have sold out a heritage like the one Gib Regal had just sold out.

He waited patiently, and after a while Gib returned. Roma read the lease, watched while Gib signed it, then counted out $1,000. He slipped the lease into his pocket with an enigmatic smile.

Gib snatched the money from the table. His hands trembled as he stuffed it into his pocket. He ducked his head and almost ran from the saloon without looking back.

X

It was exactly a week after his fight with Lew that Roma left the hotel at sunup, went to the livery barn, and hired a horse. He tied a bundle behind the saddle containing food enough for two days, and a couple of blankets wrapped in a slicker. Leaving town, he discovered that he could ride without too much pain by holding his horse to a walk and letting his injured foot dangle limply beside the stirrup.

In the days that had passed since he'd obtained the lease, he had heard from his trail boss, Dave French. French estimated that the herd would arrive in Medicine Lodge three days from now, which would put it at .45's southern boundary on the day after tomorrow.

Roma was well aware of the unsteadiness of the ground on which he stood. He knew Lew Stark was an unpredictable quantity. Lew might tolerate the lease and go to court to have it outlawed, or he might move swiftly and violently against Roma and his men. And Roma didn't like to gamble this way. He liked things certain, liked his cards marked so there was no chance of losing. In this instance, however, he had no choice. He'd done the best he could. If Lew Stark chose to attack, he would have to fight. But he'd not tell French and the others that his lease was shaky or illegal. He'd let them think Lew was trying to cheat him. They'd fight a hell of a lot better if they thought that.

He wished, though, that he'd been able to move in sooner while Lew was still preoccupied with the old man's death and funeral. If there were only some way now to distract Stark's attention from what was going on at .45's southern line. If there were only some way. . . . But there wasn't. He'd just have to take his chances and hope Lew didn't find out .45 was being invaded until the invasion was complete, until he and his men had a chance to scatter the herd and get set.

He realized, too, that he was taking a chance in crossing .45. Lew Stark had threatened to kill him if he caught him on .45 again. Still, it wasn't likely Stark would see him. The ranch was big, and if Roma was careful, he'd probably get across all right. If he was seen, he had the revolver strapped to his thigh and the Winchester repeater in the boot. He used both very well.

The morning hours passed. Roma was not familiar with .45, and so followed a two-track wagon road for the better part of the morning, not knowing where it led, but favoring it because it was smooth and reasonably level. Traveling it was easier on his foot than cutting straight across country.

At noon, he sighted a shack in the distance ahead and recognized it instantly as the one in which Lew and himself had begun their fight. He reined his horse aside to detour it, then halted suddenly, frowning. Santoyo. Abruptly Roma began to smile. Santoyo had been on this land since long before old man Regal arrived, and there had been quite a bit of resentment in Medicine Lodge over the Regal brothers ordering him to leave, considering that his rights preceded theirs. But they *had* ordered him to leave. And he hadn't left.

Roma's smile widened. Here was the thing that would distract Lew Stark. Here was revenge against Lew and against that damned Mexican wench, and accomplishment of a purpose, all in one quick stroke. But it would work only if Santoyo was at home.

Keeping to the concealment of draws, Roma approached carefully. And at last he was able to sit his horse behind a low ridge two hundred yards from the shack with only his head visible above it. He stared down into the yard. The girl Natalia was out behind the house hanging up clothes. In the brilliant sunlight, with the golden land behind her and the turquoise sky above, she made a lovely picture, arms raised, head thrown back. But there was no desire in Roma as he looked at her. He hated her now. He blamed her as much as he blamed Lew Stark for his crippled foot. He glanced at her briefly, then let his eyes rove over the house and yard. He saw nothing, and a pang of disappointment struck him. Still, he had plenty of time.

He rode carefully back down the slope, as carefully dismounted. He tied his horse to a yucca clump, then limped back up the rise again, carrying his rifle. He got down and crawled the last few feet. Motionlessly he lay, the rifle poked out in front of him, and waited. Natalia finished hanging her clothes, picked up the basket, and went inside. Smoke thickened at the chimney.

A blue fly buzzed idly around Roma's head. He ignored it, as quietly fixed as a sand lizard who hoped to catch it for dinner. Only his eyes moved, shifting back and forth across the landscape. Behind him, the horse cropped grass, his movements plainly audible.

The chimney smoke thinned out. Roma began to grow tense. He guessed that Santoyo was in there, all right. Eating dinner. In a few minutes he'd probably come out on the porch for a smoke.

Time drifted away, but no one appeared. At last, impatience began to stir in Roma. He waited a moment more, then bellowed: "Santoyo!"

The cabin door opened, and Mike Santoyo came out on the porch, looking around, puzzled.

Roma figured it would be hard to identify a shouting voice from this distance, so he yelled: "You were warned to leave. Now it's too late!"

Mike reached smoothly for his rifle, leaning against the cabin wall. Roma eased his rifle into position, sighted carefully, and pulled the trigger.

He heard the bullet strike, the way he often had when he'd shot a deer. Santoyo slammed back against the cabin wall as though struck with a fist. Momentum pinned him there for an instant, then he went limp and slid down it to the ground. He sat against the wall for the briefest moment, then toppled over and sprawled out flat.

Roma was already easing back as Natalia came screaming from the door. He saw her fall to her knees beside her father. Then he was out of sight behind the rise.

He got to his feet and hobbled hurriedly to his horse. Natalia wouldn't know where the shot had come from. She'd been inside at the time. Besides, she'd be busy with her father and her grief for a few minutes. By then Roma could be long gone. He mounted with some difficulty, and reined away. He could still hear faintly the sounds of Natalia's weeping.

He gigged the horse to a trot and after a few moments urged him to a lope. The foot banged against the horse's sides and made pain shoot all the way to Roma's hip, but he didn't slacken pace. Not until he was a full five miles south of Santoyo's shack did he rein his horse back to a walk.

He was bathed with sweat. Pain had made him dizzy, had made his head light. He gripped himself, gripped his senses determinedly. He couldn't pass out now. Damn it, he wouldn't!

For several miles he fought to retain consciousness. Maybe he should have listened to Doc. Maybe he should have stayed off his foot. But the price would have been too high. French and the crew couldn't handle Lew Stark without him. To hell with the foot! He'd done the only thing he could.

Santoyo's death didn't bother him at all. It would serve a purpose—a useful one. It would mean the difference between success and failure for him. Because Santoyo's death would keep Stark busy. The sheriff and the residents of the county would blame .45 for it. J.W.'s heirs had threatened Mike Santoyo and told him to leave. Natalia would repeat the words Roma had shouted before he fired.

There would no doubt be a coroner's inquest. Members of .45's crew, Lew Stark, and the Regal brothers would be called upon to testify. Even if they weren't, they'd at least attend Santoyo's funeral. For a few days, the vast lands that belonged to

.45 would be virtually deserted. And this was all Roma wanted—a chance to take possession, scatter his cattle, and get set for trouble.

Lew was down at the blacksmith shop, shoeing a horse when Natalia rode in. He saw her coming from a long way off, riding as though the devil himself rode at her heels. Dust lifted from her horse's hoofs. She sailed him across a washout, and Lew caught and held his breath as the horse stumbled, recovered, and came on. He eased it out in a long, slow sigh. Nervousness and concern built up in him, along with an unpleasant premonition. It wasn't like Natalia to ride like that. Something must have happened to Mike.

He walked out into the open and raised an arm. She swerved her horse and came pounding toward him without slackening speed. She hauled to a plunging halt ten feet away. Dust rolled over Lew, making him cough, for the moment obscuring Natalia, who had leaped from the horse to run toward him. It cleared and he saw her face, and suddenly he knew his premonition had been right.

Her face was gray, her eyes enormous and slightly reddened from weeping. But it was not the evidences of weeping that shocked him as much as the terrible, lost expression in her eyes. She flung herself into his arms and buried her face in his shirt front. And then a spasm of weeping took her. Her body shook violently with it. His arms tightened, holding her close against him as though this could steady her and stop the violence of her trembling.

It seemed a long time before she began to quiet. When she did, Lew relaxed his arms, cupped a hand beneath her small chin, and lifted her face. "What is it? What is it, Nata?"

"It's Mike. They've killed him!"

"Where? Who?" Even in his shocked state, Lew could feel the

beginnings of a deadly anger in his heart.

"One of you . . . I don't know which one. He was shot right after dinner as he stepped out on the porch."

"One of us? What are you talking about?"

"Oh, Lew, I know it wasn't you. But it was somebody from Forty-Five. He yelled at Mike . . . said Mike had been warned to leave and now it was too late. Then I heard the shot. I ran out on the porch and Mike was dead." Tears welled again into her enormous, liquid eyes.

"Recognize the voice?"

She shook her head. "I was inside, and the voice came from quite a ways off."

"Find any tracks?"

She nodded. "I circled before I came here. I found the place he left his horse and the place he laid down so he could see down into the yard without being seen himself."

"Where'd the tracks lead?"

"South. But that doesn't mean anything, Lew. He could have turned and come back here at any time."

Lew nodded. He asked: "Where's Mike now?"

She looked at him piteously. "I got him inside and up on the bed. Oh, Lew! What am I going to do? I loved him. He was so good and I loved him so!"

He pulled her head against his chest and patted her back awkwardly. He said evenly: "For now, go in the house. Stay with Leona. I'm going to find Mike's killer."

Keeping an arm around her, he walked with her to the wide front gate. He took her into the coolness of the house.

Leona was in the kitchen, supervising the cleaning of the stove. There were smudges of soot on her nose and forehead, and her hands were covered with it.

Lew said: "Natalia's here. Mike's been killed. Go out and stay with her, will you?"

"Mike killed? How?"

"Shot. Murdered on his own porch. Natalia thinks it was one of us."

"Oh, no!" Leona's face had paled with shock, but that passed in an instant, and then her eyes filled with compassion. "The poor child. Of course I'll stay with her." She turned to go, then swung to stare at Lew. "What are you going to do?"

"I'm going to find Mike's killer."

"You think it was one of J.W.'s sons, don't you?"

"That's what I'm going to find out. Damn them, if one of them did do this. . . ." He stopped. Then he turned and left the house through the kitchen door.

The anger that had been born in him a few moments before was growing now, and he had to beat it down savagely to clear his mind. This was no time to go off half-cocked. This was the time to think.

For a moment he considered riding to Mike's and picking up the trail. Then he shook his head. Chances were, whoever had done the killing had circled and returned to town. Tracking would prove nothing, for the tracks would be lost in the press of tracks near town. Besides, it was an hour to Mike's place. Another two or three hours would be required to track the suspect as far as town. And even if the tracks did not lead to Medicine Lodge, dark would come before Lew caught up with the killer. No, the best course was to go straight to town and find out where the Regal brothers had been at the time of the killing, which must have been a little more than an hour ago, about 1:00.

Besides, Joe Riker had to be notified. Funeral arrangements must be made. And if Lew did not find out what he needed to know in town, he could take up the trail tomorrow. There was hardly a cloud in the sky and it hadn't rained since a week ago when he and J.W. had been caught in the storm. Nothing would obscure the trail.

He roped a horse out of the corral and saddled quickly. Then he rode to the bunkhouse and called Ortiz. "Finish shoeing that horse for me, will you, Ortiz? I've got to go to town."

Ortiz nodded, and headed for the blacksmith shop. Lew spurred away and thundered north toward town across the rolling land.

Now he could let his anger rise unchecked. Now he could promise himself that whoever had killed Mike Santoyo would pay before the day was done. But the feeling of emptiness, of loss, begun with the passing of J.W., had grown stronger. Even .45 looked different to him. For .45 had been more than land in Lew Stark's mind. It had been two men besides—J.W. Regal and Mike Santoyo—and now both were gone. Both were gone and only land was left.

XI

It was almost 5:00 p.m. when Lew rode into Medicine Lodge. He rode first to Regal Street and drew rein before the small, white church. Nestling under its larger bulk was the minister's house.

Lew went up the walk and knocked. John Jennings himself answered the door. Lew said, without preamble: "Mike Santoyo has been shot. I wonder if you'd take care of things . . . funeral arrangements and all. His daughter's pretty upset."

Jennings was a tall, cadaverous-looking man. Lew hadn't often attended his services, not liking the man's almost fanatical way of roaring from the pulpit. But there was a surprising amount of humanity in Jennings, and it came out now. "The poor child. Where is she now?"

"At Forty-Five."

"And the body?"

"At Mike's place. She managed to get him inside and up

onto one of the beds."

Jennings nodded. "I'll go immediately. I'll see Natalia, and then go and sit with the body."

Lew nodded. "Thanks. I expect Riker will notify the coroner. Likely they'll both come out in the morning."

He turned and went back down the walk. Mounting, he rode to Riker's office. For once, Riker was in. The office was baking hot from the late afternoon sun beating against its back wall. Riker had both doors open, but no breeze stirred through the room. Riker sat in his swivel chair with his feet up on the desk.

Lew said: "Mike Santoyo's been murdered."

The change in Riker's expression was hardly noticeable, but Lew knew the news hit him hard. Riker, J.W. Regal, and Mike Santoyo had been the county's three oldest inhabitants. They'd been friends, though not the regular-get-together kind of friends.

Riker put his feet carefully on the floor. His mouth was grim and angry. "Who did it?"

Lew shrugged. "I don't know. I haven't been over there. Natalia brought me the news."

"How'd it happen?"

"Somebody yelled at Mike while he was eating dinner or just as he was finishing. Said he'd been warned to leave and now it was too late. Mike went out on the porch and was shot with a rifle from ambush."

Riker peered intently at Lew's face. "I understand Ira told Mike to leave, and that Guy backed him up."

Lew shrugged. "That's what I heard."

"But you don't know anything about it?"

"Only what Mike told me at J.W.'s funeral."

Riker was silent for several moments while he packed and lit his pipe. He looked indolent, relaxed, almost as though he didn't care, but Lew knew his mind was working. Through a cloud of pipe smoke, Riker peered at him. "Where were you when Mike was killed?"

Lew felt anger leap in his mind. But he said calmly enough: "At Forty-Five."

"Witnesses?"

Lew nodded. He said angrily: "That stymies you, doesn't it? You figured I'd make a good suspect. I've known Mike since I was five and I was practically raised with Natalia. But I'm a sorehead about Forty-Five. You figure I want to get even with the Regal brothers at any cost. What the hell would you have done if I'd been out riding and couldn't have proved where I was? Thrown me in jail?"

Riker's face flushed. He started to speak, but Lew wasn't through. "You're hoping you don't have to make things unpleasant for any of the Regal brothers over this, aren't you? Unless maybe it's Max. He's too stupid to be interested in politics. Only you're stymied there, too. Max was at Forty-Five all day. I know. I had him working on J.W.'s old rifle."

Riker's flush deepened painfully, and Lew knew he had put his finger on Riker's thoughts. He said disgustedly: "You just sit here, Joe, and play politics. Get together with the coroner in the morning and go out to Mike's place. I'll get the killer. For me it'll be a pleasure, no matter who it turns out to be. I'm not worried about hurting anybody's feelings. I'm not coming up for reëlection next year."

Riker's flush faded. He came halfway to his feet, then sank back. He looked up at Lew, his eyes smoldering. He asked: "Are you proud of all *your* thoughts? Do you always think the right thing and do the right thing? I'll get Mike's killer, no matter who he is. But I'm damned if I think there's anything wrong in hoping it won't cost me my job."

Lew felt a touch of shame. He said: "No, I guess there isn't. I'm sorry." He stared at Riker a moment more. "The thing is, I'm going to stay mad until he's caught. And you aren't even mad any more."

Riker didn't answer. He was staring at his boots. Lew walked to the door and went out without looking back.

Mounting, he rode first to the bank. He climbed the stairs to Will Robinson's office.

He met Robinson just inside the door, shrugging into his coat. Ira was across the room, removing the elastic bands from his sleeves preparatory to going home himself. Lew said: "Both of you been here all afternoon?"

Robinson looked faintly puzzled, but he nodded. "All day, in fact. Why?"

"Mike Santoyo's been shot, and Ira threatened him."

Ira's eyes blazed. He came across the room, his face twisted with hate. "God damn you, Lew!"

Lew looked straight into his eyes. "Shut up."

Ira did. His eyes didn't stop hating Lew but there seemed to be a secret triumph in them and this puzzled Lew.

Lew asked: "Where was Guy today? And Gib?"

Robinson said: "Gib's gone. Left on the stage two days ago."

Surprise touched Lew, surprise that bordered on amazement. Now why would Gib . . . ? He shoved his puzzlement aside. He said: "Guy?"

Robinson said: "I saw him at noon in the boarding-house dining room."

The tension and expectancy drained out of Lew. He felt limp and weak, and puzzled. Every one of the Regal brothers was in the clear, with the possible exception of Gib. He could have left town on the stage two days ago and come back soon after. But that couldn't be checked without spending a lot of time on it, time that Lew simply didn't have. He growled—"Thanks, Will."—and backed toward the door. He kept his eyes challengingly on Ira until he closed it. Then, scowling, he walked down the hall to the stairs.

In the street, he mounted and headed back toward .45. He'd wasted his time, coming to town. But he'd been so damned sure it was one of the brothers.

He began to think of Gib, the only suspect left. Where had Gib gotten the money to leave the country? And why had he left? Lew knew he'd been wanting to leave. He'd tried to get $1,000 from J.W. before the old man died. But why would Gib leave now? He was part owner in .45. Unless he'd peddled his interest to someone. Lew shook his head impatiently. No use guessing about Gib.

The sun went down and dusk crept across the land. Lew didn't push his horse, knowing he had all night if he needed it. But he was anxious to see Natalia, anxious to talk with her. There might be something she'd forgotten in her agitation, something that would put him on the right track. Hell, if one of the Regal brothers hadn't done the killing, he couldn't imagine who had. Mike Santoyo hadn't had any enemies. And Lew couldn't swallow the suspicion he'd had earlier of Gib. Gib had no reason for wanting Mike dead. Gib hadn't been in on ordering Mike to leave. All Gib wanted was to get away from his brothers, from .45, from the town that knew him so well.

It was dark when Lew rode into sight of .45. The house was ablaze with light. There was lamplight streaming from the windows of Max's room.

Lew put his horse into the corral, hung his saddle on the fence. Then he walked to the house. About day after tomorrow there'd be a coroner's inquest. He and the Regal brothers would be expected to attend. So would the crew members of .45. Both Riker and Johnson, the coroner, would want to question them.

Lew's head was beginning to ache. He went along the gallery to the kitchen door and stepped inside. Natalia was alone in the kitchen.

Lew hung his hat on a nail, studying her with sympathetic

eyes. She seemed to have conquered her grief to some extent at least. Her face was composed, though her eyes were still somewhat red from weeping. She looked at him questioningly. He shook his head. "Ira was with Robinson all day, and Robinson saw Guy at noon in the boarding house. Gib left town two days ago."

A small frown appeared on her smooth forehead. "Then who could it have been? Mike had no enemies."

Lew shook his head. "I don't know. Can you think of anything . . . anything at all? Have any of the crew been bothering you? Has Mike had a run-in with any of them?"

She shook her head. "Oh, some of them have been around once or twice. They drop by at noon to eat dinner, or they stop for water sometimes. But none of them ever get hard to handle. And Mike certainly hasn't quarreled with any of them."

Lew looked at her closely. He knew suddenly that he'd been blind where Natalia was concerned. He'd been thinking of her as a girl and she wasn't a girl at all. She wasn't his sister, either, even though they had grown up together. It had taken that moment a week ago after the fight with Roma to make him fully aware of her as a woman. Now he felt a vast tenderness toward her, and pity for her loss.

She met his eyes and looked hastily away, seeming to sense his thoughts. She asked: "Have you eaten yet?"

"No."

"Then sit down, for heaven's sake. I'll have it on in a minute."

He crossed to the sink and pumped a basinful of water. He washed his hands and face and dampened his hair. He ran a comb through it carelessly and turned.

Natalia was passing, and he collided with her. He put out his hands to catch her. He saw the lost, frightened look in her eyes and caught her to him. She was warm and soft, and trembling.

Without looking at him she whispered: "Lew, I'm lost. What

am I going to do without Mike?"

He felt helpless. He wanted to comfort her, but he knew it wasn't possible. There was no comfort but time for her loss.

He heard the door move and looked up. With Natalia still in his arms, he stared over the top of her head and saw Leona in the doorway. Leona's face was dead white, her mouth a compressed line. Fury blazed from her eyes. Then, without a word, she slammed the door and he heard her footsteps retreating across the living room behind it. He heard her steps on the stairs, and something that sounded like a sob. . . .

He released Natalia thoughtfully. Natalia's eyes showed hurt.

Lew said, aware that his voice was defensive: "It isn't what you're thinking. She was J.W.'s wife, and as far as I'm concerned, she still is."

Natalia's eyes held a sparkle of tears. "Lew, I'm sorry. I'm sorry and ashamed for what I thought. I ought to know you better than that."

He grinned ruefully. "Forget it." He was remembering Riker's words and the thought behind them: *Are you proud of all your thoughts?* Lew wasn't. No one ever is. He smiled ruefully at Natalia. "Come on, girl. Get me some grub before I starve to death."

XII

Leona was shocked beyond belief at seeing Natalia in Lew's arms. For an instant she was frozen, unable to move, unable to think. It was as though a numbing blow had been struck upon her head as she stepped through the doorway. But the numbness lasted only a moment. Then came rage, so terrible it chilled her and made her body tremble. She wanted to cross the kitchen and tear Natalia from Lew's arms. She wanted to claw, and bite, and kick. Instead, she turned and went back out of the kitchen. She ran across the big living room and raced up the stairs. A wild sob tore from her throat.

Into her bedroom she went, into the room she had shared with J.W. and which she'd hoped to share with Lew. She flung herself down on the bed, her fingers digging claw-like into the covers.

Nervously, then, she sprang up. She seized a vase and flung it savagely at the wall. It shattered.

She paced back and forth, hands clenched, nails digging into her palms. Damn him! God damn him to hell! He wouldn't touch her, but he'd touch that damned little Mexican piece quick enough. . . . Back and forth, back and forth. Sound died in the courtyard and outside the walls. Lamps winked out. But Leona's burned on.

She was thirty-five years old. Lew was thirty. Not an unbridgeable gap. She was attractive, hot-blooded. And Natalia. What was she? Slim—you could almost call her gaunt. No. Maybe that wasn't strictly true. Natalia was youthful, alive, virginal. These things attracted men.

Leona herself had been too wanton, too inviting with Lew. She'd offered herself to Lew on any terms he wished. She'd have given herself to him at any time, in any place, under any circumstances. And damn him, he knew it. Knowing it, he didn't value her. Leona's hands pressed against her flat belly. It was like a fire burning in her, this need for Lew.

She crossed the room and blew out her lamp. She went to the window and looked outside. A moon hung halfway up the eastern sky, magnified by dust in the air, made yellow by it, too. A longing so poignant that its hurting beset Leona. Daydreaming, she thought of Lew, and her imagination began to play. Realizing what she was doing, her face flushed hotly in the darkness. Her thoughts returned helplessly to Natalia Santoyo in Lew Stark's arms. And with those thoughts came hatred.

She undressed and slipped a nightgown over her head. She

lay down on the top of the bed, not bothering to get under the covers. Her eyes stared up at the ceiling, unblinking, tortured. She closed them and tried to sleep, but the fires inside her burned on. Tense and still she lay, for nearly an hour.

Then, as wide awake as ever, she sprang to her feet. In her nightgown, she went into the hall and down the stairs. Outside on the gallery she paused. Her skin was burning. Shame mounted in her, but she was helpless in the face of this overpowering desire.

Her bare feet silent, she went along the gallery to the door of Lew's room. There she hesitated, her hand on the knob. What if he refused her again? What if he laughed?

Suddenly Leona hated herself. She tried to think of J.W., in his grave little more than a week. But she found herself thinking, instead, of Lew, lying on top of the bed behind the door, as she had lain on top of hers, sprawled out in sleep, his hair tousled, his breathing even and quiet. He would rouse quickly and perhaps violently, but when he found her in his arms. . . . My God, he was a man, wasn't he? The doorknob rattled faintly under Leona's shaking hand. And then she turned the knob.

The room was dark. Lew lay upon the top of the bed as she had imagined him. His breathing was regular, even. She closed the door silently behind her. She crept across the room, desire mounting to an unbelievable pitch.

Suddenly Lew sat up. The bedsprings creaked. He moved like a cat, rolling and snatching his gun from the holster hanging with the cartridge belt on the bedpost. Leona heard the hammer click.

She screamed: "No, Lew, no!"

He froze for a moment, then flung the revolver down on the pillow. "What the hell are you doing here?" His voice was irritable.

"I couldn't sleep." She went over and sat beside him on the

bed. Her thigh touched his.

Lew got up nervously, crossed the room, and opened the door. He said: "Go on back to bed. Go back to your room."

"Lew, please. . . ."

He swung angrily to face her. She couldn't see his face, but she could imagine the expression it wore. There would be disgust there, revulsion. She caught herself thinking of Natalia, wondering what Lew would have done had it been Natalia instead of herself who had come to him in the night. Fury made her wild. She sprang to her feet. She screeched at him, screamed insults and curses. Lew stood, shocked and dumb.

Footsteps ran along the gallery, almost silent except for the faint sounds of loose gravel under them. Max burst in the door.

"What the hell? What's going on?"

Leona flung herself at him, flung herself into his arms. She was weeping suddenly, and wildly hysterical. "Max! Max, for God's sake get me out of here. Get me away from Lew!" A low rumble sounded in Max's throat. He pushed Leona aside and took a step toward Lew. Lit by moonlight streaming in the open door, he was monstrous as an ape, and as menacing.

Leona flung herself in front of him. She seized his thick forearms in her two hands. "Not now, Max, please! Just get me away! Just get me away!"

Max hesitated, and finally turned. Holding her elbow, he steered her out the door. The last thing Lew heard was the diminishing sound of her hysterical weeping, and the deep rumble of Max's outraged, comforting voice.

For a while he stood numbly in the center of the room, staring at the open door. Sleep was still not completely gone from his mind. But a few short minutes had elapsed since that dim sixth sense had awakened him and made him reach for his gun. Good God, wasn't there enough trouble on .45 without Leona making more?

He went over and sat down on the edge of the bed. His mind began to comprehend the night's happenings and their certain consequences. To anyone but Max, it would have been obvious from Leona's presence in Lew's room in her nightgown that there was no question of attempted rape. But to Max's twelve-year-old mind. . . .

Lew scowled. Max worshiped Leona. It wouldn't be in him to question anything she said. Regardless of logic, he would believe her, no matter how unbelievable her story happened to be.

Lew knew suddenly that if he wanted to take up the trail of Mike Santoyo's killer, he had better leave now. As soon as Max got Leona calmed down, he'd be back. He'd be back and all his liking and respect for Lew would be gone. All he'd want would be to kill. And Max was so damned powerful, so monstrous, that no ordinary man could stand up against him. Lew would be faced with two alternatives. Letting Max kill him by trying to fight with his hands, or killing Max with a gun in defense of his own life. Both were intolerable alternatives. Lew wasn't about to let Max kill him. And he didn't want to kill Max for something that wasn't Max's fault.

He shrugged fatalistically. He got up and slipped on his pants. He shrugged into a shirt, then sat down again and pulled on his boots. Standing, he belted his gun around his hips.

He had an odd feeling of premonition that was probably caused by the things that had happened. It wasn't over. There was more trouble coming. The odds against Lew were steadily increasing. Leona had championed him, had insisted that he stay on as foreman of .45. Now she wanted him dead—wanted him broken and maimed between Max's powerful hands. The time was getting short—Lew's time for staying here on .45. The chances of holding .45 together were growing slimmer every day.

Lew crammed his hat down on his head and went out onto the moonlit gallery. There was a lamp burning in the living room.

He headed for the corral, thinking of J.W., marveling at the state things had gotten into in the short week since J.W.'s death. And, judging from appearances, things were going to get worse. At present, however, Lew had only one objective—to reach Santoyo's before dawn and take up the trail of the killer. When that was done, he could work at his other problems in turn.

He roped a horse out of the corral, led him over to the barn, and threw on his saddle. Cinching down, he mounted and rode out toward Mike Santoyo's place. He didn't like himself for running away. In Max's mind it would be a confession of guilt. He grinned wryly to himself.

The moon climbed across the sky and began to settle toward the western horizon as he rode. At 2:00 he came in sight of Mike Santoyo's shack. The light in it startled him until he remembered that John Jennings, the town's minister, was sitting with Mike's body.

He rode up to the shack, dismounted, and tied. It seemed incredible to him that so much could have happened in less than twenty-four hours, indeed scarcely more than twelve. Mike had been alive yesterday noon. Now he was dead and Lew's place at .45 was gone. He knew he'd go back to pick up his things. He also knew he couldn't stay.

He knocked on the door and stepped inside. Jennings was sitting in a rocker, the Bible in his lap. He got up at once. "Hello, Lew. Want some coffee?"

"I could sure use it."

Jennings went over to the stove. He brought Lew a steaming cup of thick black coffee. Lew sipped it gratefully.

Jennings studied him. "Going to take up the trail of the killer?"

Lew nodded.

"Isn't that the sheriff's job?"

Lew shrugged.

Jennings quoted sonorously: " 'Vengeance is mine, saith the Lord.' "

Lew glanced at him. "You reckon the Lord is going to catch that killer?"

"The Lord moves in mysterious ways."

Lew said: "There's another saying that you're forgetting. The Lord helps those that help themselves. I reckon the Lord don't want a man to sit on his haunches while he waits for the Lord to do all the work. Hell, man, I'm not going to execute Mike's killer. I just want to catch him."

He finished his coffee and got up. He stared at the windows, which were beginning to turn slightly gray.

He crossed the room and went into the bedroom. Mike Santoyo lay on the bed, covered with a sheet. Lew pulled the sheet back and looked at his face.

He had needed this. He had needed to see this man who had always been so strong, so much a part of the land, so much a part of Lew's own life. He had needed to see Mike helpless, a cold lump of dead flesh, eyes closed, the life and strength gone from his wiry body. He felt anger rise—outraged anger because this was so useless, so wholly without point. Mike had lived as a tame animal does, hurting no one, making no enemies, only friends. Now he was dead, shot down from ambush without a chance to defend himself.

Lew looked at the gray seeping in the window. His mouth was a thin, straight line, his eyes were hard. It was time to go.

XIII

Outside, he waited perhaps half an hour beside his horse until the light became strong enough. Then he mounted and began a wide circle of the place.

He crossed his own tracks, those of Natalia's and the preacher's before he found what he sought, the tracks of a single horse riding in from the direction of town. He followed their course and found where the rider had dismounted. He was hurrying, and the light was only strong enough to make out the tracks themselves. Otherwise, he would most certainly have noticed the way the tracks dragged, the way one of them was oddly smudged. He would have known his man was Alameda Roma, whose foot was injured and tied up in heavy bandages.

He found the single cartridge Roma had jacked out of his rifle after killing Mike. Satisfied, he mounted and followed the circuitous trail Roma had made in leaving here. Now the light was stronger. The east was faintly pink. Lew urged his horse to a trot, slowing only when necessary to pick out the trail crossing a stretch of hardpan or a stand of thick grass.

The sun came up and rose across the sky. Lew rode steadily, ever southward, growing more and more puzzled as time went on. A new suspicion was beginning to grow in his mind. He was beginning to wonder if Ira and Guy had not hired the killing done, whether the killer, having done his job, was not now on his way out of the country to safety. If he was, he could easily be a hundred miles away. He could be forever out of Lew Stark's reach.

Lew caught himself hurrying. Wherever possible, he let his horse lope easily along. He took to guessing at the trail rather than following it slavishly, and found he was able to make better time, for the trail scarcely deviated from its straight southern course.

Noon came, but Lew did not stop. In midafternoon he halted to rest his horse and let him drink at a narrow stream. He was getting close to .45's southern boundary now. Ahead he could see the ragged buttes that marked the beginning of a badlands in which there was little grass and no water at all. A natural boundary and a good one. No one lived in the badlands and cattle wouldn't cross it unless they were driven.

The edge of the badlands lay four or five miles ahead. Lew got down and eased to the top of a low rise. He lay there on his stomach for ten minutes or more, scanning the land ahead. He saw nothing save for a couple of small antelope bands, grazing in the distance.

He went on as the sun dropped toward the mountains in the west. He still had several hours to follow the trail. He might, with luck, get through the badlands before dark caught up with him. He began to hurry even more, and, hurrying, his vigilance relaxed.

Roma had made it to the edge of the badlands the day before as evening fell. He had camped at the edge of the badlands, eaten a cold supper, and gone immediately to bed. His foot had weakened him and made him irritable, and so he slept little during the night. Wakeful, he stared at the stars.

Doubt was beginning to stir in him. Perhaps he'd been wrong in extending himself so far, in leaving so much to chance. It had been easy enough, in the drought-stricken areas of Texas, to get together a herd on trust. But he still owed their owners for them even if the price was ridiculously low. And he still had to pay his crew.

The trouble was he hadn't anticipated any difficulty in leasing range. And he'd encountered nothing else but trouble. He knew that more was ahead. Santoyo's murder was bound to have repercussions and .45 would fight for their range unless Lew Stark could in some way be eliminated.

He frowned to himself. The killing of Santoyo had been smart in a sense. It would give him the time he so desperately needed to scatter his herd on .45 and get ready to fight. Running away, leaving a plain trail, had not been smart, as he realized now. Tomorrow someone might pick it up and follow it. What he should have done was turn around and return to town. And then start out afresh along a different route.

Killing Santoyo had been a spur-of-the-moment decision that he hadn't adequately thought out. He realized that he'd better think it out now and plan for the eventualities that might occur. Another rain like the one a week ago would put him in the clear. But the sky was clear. He couldn't count on that. And how about the sheriff? Would the sheriff gather a posse and take up the trail? Probably he would.

Tomorrow, then, he'd better get up at dawn and proceed to lose himself. The badlands were loaded with hardpan and rocky ground. A man could lose his trail easily enough in there. Then, after a day of hiding trail in the badlands, he'd return here, conceal himself and his horse, and watch. He'd find out if anyone was on his trail. If the posse was no larger than two or three, he could probably take care of them at long range with his rifle, just as he had Santoyo.

He went to sleep then, and awoke at dawn. He ate a hasty cold breakfast, saddled, mounted, and rode into the badlands.

All day he trailed through the badlands. He wound down rocky draws, over ridges of hardpan and shale. He left not a single track to betray the course he had taken.

In midafternoon, satisfied that he had eliminated chance of pursuit and capture, he returned to the edge of the badlands, still without leaving sign behind. At its very edge, he tied his horse on the rocky bottom of a wash and afoot, with difficulty, climbed the highest knoll for miles around and scanned the land to the north.

He saw nothing, but he did not leave. Instead, he settled down to doze and wait, from time to time resuming his inspection of the trail he had made the day before. At last, around

131

4:00, he saw the single rider moving along it.

Now he was glad for the pains he had taken, for he recognized, even at a distance of half a mile, the distinctively tall, slim figure of Lew Stark. Carefully he eased his rifle up beside him. He jacked a cartridge into the chamber.

The trail passed within three hundred yards of this spot. Too long a distance for shooting with complete accuracy. Still, there was no reason why he couldn't make a hit. He'd have five or six chances before Lew could reach cover. It ought to be enough.

So he waited, tension building in him as he did, and fury because of the continuing pain in his foot. If only Lew Stark had been reasonable and agreed to lease him range, all this could have been avoided. But Lew Stark hadn't been reasonable. He had refused, and now would have to die. Roma had everything he had been able to earn and save in a lifetime tied up in this cattle venture. It was his last chance. If he lost out now, he'd never have anything. He'd have lived his life for exactly nothing.

Lew came closer, studying the ground, hurrying his horse as though he hoped to get through the badlands before dark came. Roma smiled. Cautiously he eased the rifle muzzle out before him. He brought the piece to his shoulder and let it bear on Lew.

Looking at Lew, the hatred, the fury born of his fight with Lew at Santoyo's cabin came surging back. He realized his hands were trembling slightly. He realized that something was jumping unpleasantly in the pit of his stomach.

Unaware he was being watched, Lew came closer. Once he lifted his head and looked around.

Roma's heart almost stopped as Lew's gaze seemed to rest on him for a fraction of a second. Then Lew's glance dropped to the ground again.

Roma's finger tightened on the trigger. The range was now

only slightly over three hundred yards. His mind calculated rapidly. At three hundred yards the bullet would drop about a foot. If he aimed at Lew's head, he was almost certain to gut-shoot the man.

Lew was directly beneath him now. Roma steadied his bead and squeezed steadily on the trigger.

Flame and smoke shot from the gun muzzle. The piece bucked against Roma's shoulder. He heard the bullet strike. Lew's horse jumped, and Lew went out of the saddle on the left side.

The horse ran a dozen steps. Behind him and beneath him, Roma could see Lew's legs, keeping pace. When the horse went down, Lew dropped with him. The horse lay still and there was no movement behind him.

For an instant, Roma didn't move. He had failed. Damn it, he had failed! He'd hit the god-damned horse and missed Lew altogether. The way Lew had so instantly reacted told Roma that here was a formidable opponent. There'd been no hesitation in Lew. The instant he'd heard the rifle crack, he'd gone out of his saddle. He'd had presence of mind enough to pace the horse until he fell, so that when he did, he'd have cover from which to fight back.

For a few moments panic stirred in Roma's mind. His cattle were due tomorrow. And with Lew nosing around. . . . Then he began to smile. Lew wouldn't be nosing around. All he had to do was leave, make his way carefully through the badlands to where he intended to meet the cattle on the other side. Lew, left afoot thirty miles from home, would have no alternative but to walk. In high-heeled boots, that would take him all night and probably most of tomorrow. Roma began to smile. This was not working out so badly at all.

He eased back out of sight and carefully went to his horse. He mounted and rode out, never leaving rocky ground. He was

well into the badlands before Lew even poked his head above
the body of the dead horse.

Lew waited about thirty minutes before he moved. Probably the
ambusher realized that he wasn't hurt. But he couldn't be sure.
The man may have been far enough away so that he'd believed
Lew's foot was hung in the stirrup. He might even believe that
Lew was dead. If he did, he'd be along pretty soon to check.

But when a half hour had passed with no sign of the ambusher, Lew realized he wasn't coming. He poked his head cautiously up over the body of the horse. Nothing happened. He
raised up so that his head and shoulders showed. Then he stood
up. Still nothing happened.

Leaving the horse and carrying his rifle at ready, he climbed
the hill. The attacker had been careful about sign, leaving only a
matted place in the grass where he had lain. Lew walked to the
bottom and found horse droppings where his horse had stood.
Beyond that there was nothing.

Disgusted, Lew went back to where his dead horse lay. For a
few moments he stood there, fuming. Here he was, helpless,
thirty miles from home, with no alternative but to walk. Sure,
he could follow his own trail back on the chance that he'd meet
the sheriff, but he had little hope he would. He had an idea
Riker didn't really want to find Santoyo's killer. He had an idea
Riker didn't want to know who it was. Riker was afraid it might
turn out to be one of the Regal brothers or someone hired by
them.

He scowled blackly, then with a little shrug turned and, carrying his rifle, headed north toward home. He knew now what
he would have found had he reached the badlands. He would
have run completely out of trail. Whoever he had been following, whoever had shot at him, would have hidden his trail in the
badlands.

So he puzzled at motive. Why had the killer picked Santoyo? Why had he fled south, leaving so plain a trail? Had the whole thing been only a ruse to draw Lew away from .45 to a place where he could be killed? The idea intrigued him because it was the most probable solution that had yet occurred to him. But who was behind it? The Regal brothers? Probably. They were the only ones who could possibly have any reason for wanting both Lew Stark and Mike Santoyo dead.

Mile after mile he tramped, steadily, tirelessly. The sun dropped behind the mountains in the west and the sky turned gray with dusk. The way seemed endless, and when full dark fell, Lew realized he had covered less than five miles. His feet ached from walking in the high-heeled boots. His legs were stiff and sore from the unaccustomed exercise. He sat down and ruefully rolled a smoke.

He contemplated the ruins of the life he'd had on .45 regretfully. J.W. and Mike Santoyo were dead, leaving a void in Lew's life that nothing would ever quite fill. There was Max to face upon his return to .45. There was Santoyo's killer, still at large, still unknown. Disgust with the whole business came over him. Why was he trying so hard to hold .45 together for J.W.'s sons? Why? They sure as hell didn't appreciate it, and they never would.

But, looking around him at the brooding, darkening land, he knew. This was more than land, more than money, more than power. It was a monument of sorts; it was the sum and substance of both Lew's life and that of J.W. Regal's. It was home and Lew would go on fighting tenaciously for it. Even if he were forcibly evicted from it, he'd go on fighting. Not to possess it. Not even to live on it. But only to see it remain a single piece of land under a single brand. He'd fight for that until they laid him in his grave.

XIV

At dawn, Lew altered course, swinging toward .45. He supposed that Mike's funeral would take place today at his little cabin, and regretted his inability to be present. But he knew that by the time he could walk there, it would be all over. Besides, he hated facing Natalia and admitting failure. And then there was the thing between Max and himself, which he did not want to erupt in the presence of a large crowd.

Walking steadily in spite of his sore feet and aching legs, he reached .45 in midafternoon. His boots were worn almost through; he was near exhaustion.

Yet in spite of exhaustion, he knew he must face Max as soon as Max returned from Santoyo's funeral. He wondered if time had dimmed Max's rage. He wondered if, by any chance, reason had filtered through the outrage in Max's undeveloped mind. He doubted it.

He dreaded facing Max. It was all so damned stupid. Max was wrong, but was convinced that he was right. Briefly Lew hated Leona. How could she have done such a thing? Couldn't she see the consequences of it? Didn't she know that somebody was going to get killed? Or didn't she care? Lew didn't believe that of her. She wasn't bad, not basically. She'd just been out of her mind with rage.

Lew stopped first at the pump by the cook shack and took a long, cold drink. He stuck his head under the gushing spout and let the water soak his head and neck. Then he limped toward the house.

He was relieved to see that nobody had returned as yet from Mike's funeral. The place was deserted.

He went to his room and pulled off his boots. He lay back on the bed and sighed with relief. God, he was tired! He could lie here and sleep for a week. But there'd be no sleep for him. Not today. Not until he'd had it out with Max.

Desperation touched him. What in God's name was he going to do? He couldn't kill Max. He couldn't use a gun on him, knowing Max was only fighting for what he intensely believed to be right. But neither was he going to let Max get those monstrous hands on him. He wasn't going to let Max kill him.

He got up and paced back and forth in his stockings. The socks hung on his feet in rags, letting his toes stick through.

He heard them coming and hastily yanked off the worn-out socks and replaced them with a clean pair. He found another pair of boots, slightly larger than the ones he had worn out, and pulled them on.

Tension kept building in him, intolerable tension at the intolerable situation with which he was faced. He heard a buggy roll into the courtyard and, going to his door, stared out.

Afternoon sunlight washed the yard. Max held the reins of the buggy horse. He drove up to the house, looped the reins around the whip stock, and got ponderously down.

He went around the buggy and put up his hand to help Leona. Lew studied her face. Her eyes were red from crying, perhaps because of Santoyo's death, perhaps because of shame over what she had done. Lew didn't know, and discovered he didn't particularly care. He stepped out the door to the shaded gallery. There was anger in him now, and it showed in his face, in his narrowed eyes. He said: "Leona. It's time for a little truth. Tell Max what really happened the other night."

Startled, Max swung around. Leona's face went dead white. Max's eyes raged; his mouth worked. His great hands made fists, relaxed, and clenched again. Like a great bear, he shambled toward Lew.

Lew's voice was a whip. "Damn it, Leona, tell him! Tell him before I have to kill him!"

But Leona seemed frozen where she stood. Her lips were slightly parted and her eyes were wide with terror. Suddenly

Lew knew he couldn't draw his gun. He couldn't stand here and cold-bloodedly shoot down Max. And wounding him wouldn't help because Max would come on anyway. Only death would stop him. Only a bullet in the heart could put him down.

Max made a wordless growl in his throat. His eyes blazed hatred. He looked at Lew as he might have looked at a rattler or a Gila monster, dumbly hating, dumbly wanting to destroy.

Lew said: "Max! Stop right where you are! Damn it, Leona lied. Use your head. She was wearing a nightgown. She was in my room. How the hell . . . ?"

The growl in Max's throat changed to a roar. He charged at Lew, running along the gallery toward him.

It was terrible to see so much power concentrated in one living thing, and controlled by such an undeveloped brain. Lew's hand went to his gun, touched its grips, and fell away. It wasn't in him to kill Max. It would be like killing a brother, like killing a child. Lew couldn't draw even if his failure to draw must cost him his life.

He side-stepped nimbly, but Max's swinging paw caught him on the side of the head. Lew's head rang. He was flung aside, as though kicked by a horse. He tumbled out into the dusty courtyard, falling and sliding for several feet.

Shaking his head, he struggled to his hands and knees. He saw Max's legs and monstrous feet coming off the gallery, coming into the courtyard after him. His arms and legs were like lead, but he forced his mind to work, forced his muscles to gather themselves. When Max was but a couple of yards away, Lew drove forward and up, all the power of his sinewy legs behind his lunge. It was no use. He was like a mouse attacking a hungry cat. But he had to try. He wasn't just going to stand and let Max have his way.

In his ears was Leona's shrill scream as his head struck Max's barrel-like body. He heard the air gust out of Max's lungs, and felt it hot upon his neck. Again one of those monstrous hands struck him and he was flung aside like a broken doll.

He lit on his shoulders, and skidded again. His head reeled; his senses were fading fast. He choked: "Max, for God's sake!"

But Max was coming again. All Lew could see as he tried to roll was Max's monstrous feet. A kind of lassitude came over Lew. Nearly twenty-four hours of steady walking, without rest, without sleep, without food, lay behind him. He was as near exhaustion as a man can be and still stay on his feet. Max had stunned him twice, and hitting Max was just like hitting the adobe wall of the house. It made no mark, left no impression. He wanted to quit, but he found it wasn't in him to quit. By its own volition, his body was rising, his hands clenching, and he was driving forward to meet Max.

Max's face blurred. The outlines of his body were uncertain and vague. The sun seemed impossibly hot against Lew's head and neck. His mouth was dry as cotton. But even now he couldn't hate. He couldn't hate and he couldn't touch his gun.

He swung, every bit of waning power he possessed behind the blow. It struck Max's cheek and didn't even rock his head. Lew's hand felt as though it were broken, but he swung again.

The blow didn't even land. Max's clenched first caught him in the middle of the chest. Pain, so sharp and excruciating that it nearly blinded him, roared through his body. He was flung back, his feet clear off the ground for nearly a yard.

This was the end. His chest felt as though it were smashed. He lit on his back, his head striking the hard-packed ground of the courtyard with a sodden thud. Lights flashed before his eyes and the sun beat mercilessly into his face. A cloud of dust, raised by his fall, drifted slowly away.

A vague notion that this had happened before came over his fuzzy thoughts. He remembered then. The day of J.W.'s funeral. All four of the Regal brothers had attacked him, but in the end it was Max who had defeated him.

Max's shadow fell over him. Lew's body tightened against the expected kick of Max's monstrous boot. The end was near now. Max would kill him quickly.

A gun roared not ten feet away. Not a pistol. Not a rifle. It was the unmistakable bellow of a shotgun. Lew guessed from the sound that both barrels must have been fired at once. Max's great figure stopped, swayed, then toppled like a giant pine. His chest was a mass of blood. He was driven sideways and fell to the ground.

Lew stared at him uncomprehendingly. He struggled to sit up. Max must have taken the full charge of both barrels straight through his chest. His shirt was shredded. His chest beneath its remnants was. . . . Lew shuddered, and turned his head.

As he did, the shotgun clattered from Leona's hands. It struck the ground and broke open. Smoke curled lazily from its gaping twin barrels.

Breathing shallowly, wincing against the pain, Lew got slowly to his feet. He looked at Leona's face. Her eyes were haunted, terrible. It was as though she were looking into the deepest pits of hell.

He pitied her, then. She had brought this on, but she was paying for it. She'd go on paying until she died.

In through the gates streamed the .45 crew. They still wore their stiff funeral finery. A few of them had apparently been in the midst of changing.

Lew said: "Wrap Max in a blanket and take him inside. One of you go to town for the sheriff."

Without looking at Leona, he staggered to his room. He closed the door and for a moment stared emptily at the wall. Where was the end to killing and death? Where was the end to hate?

He fell on the bed, shocked and numb and sick. It was a

long, long time before he went to sleep.

XV

Roma left the scene of the ambush with conflicting emotions. There was some satisfaction in the realization that Lew Stark, afoot, was powerless to prevent his invasion of .45. But he was angry with himself as well. Damn it, the distance between himself and Lew had been no more than three hundred yards. His bullet should have found its mark. Briefly he hoped it had. Lew might have been wounded. And if he had been, the distance to .45 would become an almost insurmountable obstacle.

As he rode carefully through the badlands, he promised himself that there would be another time, another place, another go at Lew. But not until he was set on .45.

The daylight hours faded as he rode through the twisting, barren maze of badlands. A waterless place—a place of eroded earth, of lifelessness. The place made a man think of death. He shivered, and wondered that he did. Was his wound festering? Was he feverish and was this the source of the chill? He felt his anger growing. Damn Lew Stark anyway! But for Lew he would be whole and well. But for Lew's refusal to lease, he would not be facing a fight as soon as it was known that he was here.

As the first stars winked overhead, Roma reached the far side of the badlands. Here, he rode to the top of a hill and stared out across the hilly land. Somewhere out there his herd was bedded down. He squinted, and at last thought he caught the gleam of a campfire in the southern distances, flickering like a yellow star lying upon the land. He fixed the direction in his mind and rode that way.

He rode up to the camp on the side away from the herd so as not to startle them. He didn't want any senseless stampedes at this stage of the game.

Several of his men watched him ride in, wary until they

141

recognized him. Then they relaxed.

Roma dismounted with difficulty and hobbled to the fire. Dave French, a short, barrel-shaped man with a red beard, greeted him with a wide grin and an outstretched hand.

"What happened to your foot?"

"Hurt it." Roma looked at him irritably and French's glance fell away. Roma glowered at the fire for an instant, then asked: "Everything all right? Any losses?"

"Not to speak of. You get the range you wanted?"

Roma said: "I've got a lease. The graze lies on the other side of that badlands north of here."

French studied him. "How many of us are you going to need?"

"All of you." Roma caught French's expression of surprise and added quickly: "For the time being, anyway. The ranch I'm leasing from is an estate. There's some bickering among the heirs."

French didn't comment. Roma stood for a few moments more, staring into the flickering fire. He wasn't hungry. He didn't want coffee. All he wanted was to lie down and get his weight off his aching foot.

He went to his horse and took down his blanket roll. He said to French: "Have someone turn my horse in with the rest."

Then he lay down, a few yards away from the fire.

But he didn't sleep immediately. There was a strange feeling of uneasiness in him that he couldn't understand. Finally, convincing himself it had been caused by the gloominess of the badlands through which he had come, he relaxed and went to sleep.

But it was neither a dreamless sleep nor an easy one. Figures out of the past kept marching through his dreams—his mother, slatternly, her huge breasts plainly outlined beneath a thin, soiled cotton dress—the drunken troopers who paraded in and out of her bed. The fights behind the stables—the epithets, the taunts. "Your ma's nothin' but a whore. An' you're nothin' but a half-breed Mex." The way the post's officers looked through him without really seeing him.

How many times had he whispered through clenched teeth: "I'll show you! I'll *be* somebody. I'll *make* you look at me."

He woke, sweating. His foot pained unbearably. He raised on an elbow, fished in his pocket for makings, and rolled a cigarette.

He was on his way, he told himself. Lush and rich with grass, .45 lay to the north, and he had a lease from one of the heirs. His herd was intact; there had been no losses. He had a crew that would fight. Why, then, was he worried? Why this unexplainable feeling of uneasiness? The answer was Lew Stark. Lew Stark would have to die.

When Lew awoke, it was dark outside. For a few moments he lay still, feeling the steady ache of his body, aware of a depression of the spirit. He remembered Max—the fight and Max's death—almost immediately. He swung his legs over the side of the bed. He had no exact idea what time it was, but supposed it must be close to midnight.

He found tobacco and crushed papers in his pocket and made a cigarette. He lit it and dragged the smoke deep into his lungs. Then he got up and stumbled out of his room onto the gallery outside.

There were lights in the house, and in Max's room. Lew went into the house by way of the kitchen and stopped at the sink to take a long, cold drink and pump water over his head. He dried himself vigorously, then went into the living room, reflectively rubbing a hand over his growth of whiskers.

Leona sat in a corner of one of the sofas. Her face was pale and drawn. Her eyes seemed sunken deep in their sockets and there were hollows beneath them. Her lips were almost gray. Lew felt an instant pity for her.

Joe Riker, the sheriff, sat across from her. He looked up at Lew. "Where'd your killer's trail lead?"

"South to the badlands."

"Where it petered out, I suppose."

Lew shook his head. "I don't know. He ambushed me at the edge of the badlands. Shot my horse out from under me. I had to hoof it home."

Riker whistled soundlessly. He was silent for a moment, then came directly to the question obviously uppermost in his mind. "Let's hear your story of what happened to Max."

Lew shot a glance at Leona. She refused to meet his eyes. He asked Riker: "What's she told you?"

"Never mind that. Just tell your story."

Lew sighed. Leona looked up then and said: "I told him the truth, Lew."

Lew said: "All right. The night Mike was killed, Leona came to my room. I was asleep. Leona and I argued and Max overheard. He came busting in and right off reached a bunch of wrong conclusions. When I got back this afternoon, he jumped me. He was trying to kill me and Leona shot him. Probably all she wanted to do was scare him but it didn't turn out that way. That's all there is."

Leona was watching his face intently. She made a ghost of a smile. "Thank you, Lew."

Riker was studying Lew, grudging respect in his eyes. He said: "That ain't exactly what Leona said, but it's close enough."

"And?"

"There'll be no charges. Max *would* have killed you. I knew him well enough to know that. And she *did* save your life. I'm pretty sure she didn't know what she was stirring up when she let Max believe you tried to . . . well, you know." Riker flushed painfully, avoiding Leona's eyes.

Leona began to cry softly.

Lew heard a horse outside, entering the courtyard. He crossed the room to the door, with a quick glance at Riker. "Sounds like more trouble for you, Joe."

But it was not someone seeking the sheriff. It was Natalia Santoyo. She dismounted at the edge of the gallery and tied her horse. She came across to the door.

Her eyes rested steadily on Lew's face, saw his weariness and discouragement, and softened with compassion. Lew said: "Come on in, Nata. Sorry I couldn't. . . ."

"I know, Lew. I know you couldn't come. Mike would have wanted you to follow those tracks. What happened?"

There seemed to be no vengefulness in her, Lew noticed. He said: "I was ambushed at the edge of the badlands. He shot my horse out from under me." He grinned slightly. "I had to walk home."

Obviously Natalia had not heard of Max's death. And he didn't want to tell her now. She said: "Manuel Sanchez rode in a little while ago. He said that a herd of cattle is moving onto Forty-Five across the badlands."

Suddenly everything fell into place in Lew's mind. Roma was the one who had shot Santoyo, the one who had shot his horse out from under him at the edge of the badlands. Now Roma was moving in. Lew looked at Riker. "That ought to be plain enough for you."

Riker was hesitating. He said: "Roma's got a lease."

"Who from?" Anger lifted in Lew.

"Gib."

"How the hell do you know?"

"I saw a copy of it in Robinson's office."

Lew's anger soared like a fire. "That lease is no good," he stormed, "and you know damned good and well it isn't. Gib had no authority to lease. Why hell, he only holds a one-eighth interest in Forty-Five."

Riker shrugged. "I don't know about that. You'll have to fight it out in court. If the lease ain't legal, I'll evict Roma."

Lew glared furiously. "Why you son-of-a-bitch! Are you in on it, too? You know damned good and well Roma killed Mike. You know he shot at me. You know he's stealing Forty-Five range. What the hell does it take to move you?"

Riker's face tightened with rage. "You can't talk to me like that!"

"I can and I will. You go on, Joe. You crawl back in your hole. If you won't take care of Roma, then, by God, I will."

He thought Riker would swing on him. Riker breathed almost inaudibly: "You do and I'll treat you like any other law-breaker. Roma's lease was obtained in good faith . . . at least we have to assume it was. And you've got no proof he was anywhere near Mike's house. Why the hell would he kill Mike anyway? He'd never seen him before in his life." He turned toward the door. "Besides that, Roma ain't going any place. He's got three thousand cattle on Forty-Five. He ain't about to run off and leave 'em."

Lew didn't answer him. His hands were trembling with rage.

Riker banged the door behind him. Lew heard his horse thunder out of the yard and knew Riker was taking out his temper on the horse.

Maybe it *was* too pat to say that because the trail of Mike's killer went south, because Roma was now moving in from the south, that they were one and the same man. Maybe it was too pat for Riker. But it wasn't for Lew.

Leona sat listlessly on the sofa, staring at nothing. Lew looked down at Natalia and smiled. "Why don't you stay here tonight?"

Her heart leaped into her eyes, but she shook her head.

Lew said: "Then I'll walk you to the gate."

She turned and went outside, and Lew followed. He was thankful for the little Mexican settlement south of the badlands,

thankful for their friendship with the Santoyos, their loyalty to
.45. Without them he wouldn't have known about Roma until it
was too late.

Natalia put a timid hand on his arm. In the semidarkness,
her eyes devoured his face. "You'll be careful, won't you, Lew?"

He pulled her roughly against him. "Of course I will." He
lowered his head and kissed her on the mouth.

Banked fires glowed and leaped like those in a forge when
the bellows blow upon them. Lew's arms tightened. Natalia's
body arched against him. He pulled away, almost breathless.

Natalia whispered: "Maybe I will stay here tonight. With you,
Lew."

His hands trembled on her arms, but his voice was firm.
"Oh, no, you won't."

"You don't want me?"

"Damn it, of course I want you."

"No more little sister stuff?" She was smiling now.

Lew's voice was hoarse. "No more little sister stuff." He
stared down at her, feeling a great tenderness for her. He said:
"You're making one hell of a catch, Nata. I won't have a thing
but the shirt on my back."

"A woman marries a man, not a collection of things."

"Oh, she does? Now who said anything about marriage?"

Her voice was light with suppressed laughter. "I did. I made
up my mind when I was eight that I was going to marry you."

Lew grinned. "And I never had a chance."

"No." She stood on tiptoe and kissed him lightly on the
mouth. The humor was gone from her now, and fear made her
eyes huge pools of darkness. "Be careful, Lew. I want you back."

"Sure. Now get on home. I'll see you tomorrow night."

She nodded uncertainly and rose lightly to her saddle. She
reined around and rode into the velvet dark. Lew turned and
tramped heavily toward his room.

Besides Roma, there were still Guy and Ira Regal to be reckoned with. They'd probably support Roma's claim if only to make things difficult for Lew. He scowled and went inside.

XVI

Lew was up at dawn, dressed, and down at the cook shack when Swede, the cook, got up. Swede was a lanky, pale-skinned man a few years older than Lew. He seldom shaved his pale whiskers, and his undershirt was gray with dirt, but his cook shack was spotless. Lew went in, found a chair, and watched while Swede, his hair tousled from sleeping, grumpily built up the fire.

As he worked, Swede growled: "Ain't the same place since the old man died. Nobody knows what they want. Nobody knows what the hell to do."

Lew grinned. He kept wondering how many men Roma had, and how the day would go. He was aware that he stood on shaky ground. Roma had a lease and the law might support it. If that happened, Lew himself would be the one guilty of committing an unlawful act. Not only that, but Lew was pretty sure none of the heirs, with the possible exception of Leona, would support him. Leona was an unknown quantity. After what had happened, Lew didn't know whether she still wanted him to stay on as foreman, or whether she wanted him to leave. When she got over the shock of killing Max, he supposed she'd let him know.

There was an odd feeling stirring in Lew, a feeling of restlessness and tension. The past week or so had been bad. Everything had turned out wrong. Without exception, everyone seemed to be opposing him or creating trouble for him. Yet he still had himself under control.

He thought of Guy's words the day of J.W.'s funeral and wondered how much had been truth, how much lies and distortions. Some of what Guy had said must have been true, for they were corroborated by J.W.'s cryptic statements before he died. J.W. had been a lawman and he probably *had* killed Lew's father. Lew frowned. From what he'd heard, his father hadn't really been a criminal. But he'd had an ungovernable temper and it had led him to killing someone. J.W. had apparently been afraid Lew possessed the same temper, afraid Lew would follow the same path his father had.

He wondered about that. On the day of the fight with Roma he *had* wanted to kill and probably would have except for J.W.'s intervention. He'd been close to killing Ira on the day of J.W.'s funeral when the brothers had jumped him. And yet he'd refused to kill Max even though refusal meant almost certain death. He shook his head confusedly.

Swede brought him a steaming mug of coffee and he sipped it thoughtfully. He began to dread the day ahead, wondering if before it was through he would be a killer just as his father had been.

The crew began to straggle in, without shirts, with their hair wet from the pump. Lew waited.

There were eight crewmen in all, and Swede, the cook. When they were all inside, seated at the long table, Lew said: "I got word last night that a man named Roma has moved about three thousand cattle onto the southern part of Forty-Five. We're going to go push him off today. I want all of you to bring rifles, plenty of ammunition, and your six-shooters. Anybody that doesn't want to go, say so now."

He waited. The faces of the men were startled, and perhaps a little tense, but nobody asked to be excused.

Lew said: "He's been on Forty-Five long enough to have gotten his cattle scattered. Likely his crew will be waiting for us."

Nobody spoke. Swede brought an enormous platter of flapjacks and another of fried beef. The men ate silently and hungrily. Lew scanned their faces, one by one.

Next to him sat Slim Clark and next to Slim, his shadow, Jess Leonard. The two were always together. Beyond Jess sat Frank Dennis and a kid called Sonny Rose.

On the opposite side of the table was oldster Dad Lloyd, his bald head gleaming, Dan Arnold, Stew Fleischman, Russ Dodge, and Dell Heckethorn.

All of them, with the exception of Sonny Rose, had been around .45 for years. Lew said: "I think Roma is the one that bushwhacked Mike, but the sheriff doesn't agree. I tracked the killer all the way to the badlands and got my horse shot out from under me for my pains. There's no telling why Roma would want Mike dead, but I still think he's our man."

He finished his breakfast, and stood up. Hearing a commotion up by the house, he went to the door. He saw two riders turning in the gate, and recognized them immediately as Guy and Ira Regal.

He turned. "When you're finished eating, saddle up. Slim, saddle a horse for me."

"Sure, Lew."

Lew stepped out into the cool morning air. The sun was rising in the east, staining a few scattered cloud layers pale pink.

Lew made a smoke and was surprised to see that in spite of the tension gripping him, his hands were steady. Then, drawing smoke deep into his lungs, he headed for the house.

Ira's and Guy's horses stood tied before the gallery. Lew doubted if they knew anything about his proposed expedition to the badlands after Roma. Probably they were here because of Max's death. Probably Max would be buried today, and they were here for that.

He walked across the gallery and entered the house. The tension kept building in him. Ira and Guy were unknown quantities at this stage of the game. They had attacked him once; they might again. Lew had a hunch they wouldn't try with their fists a second time. Next time it would be with guns.

Leona was with them in the living room. All were standing. Leona was clad in a heavy wrapper and had, apparently, just gotten out of bed. Her hair was enclosed in a gingham cap with elastic around the edges. Her face was haggard and pale. She looked ten years older than she usually did.

Lew felt an immediate pity for her. She was taking her killing of Max pretty hard. Or maybe it wasn't the killing that bothered her as much as the fact that the quarrel leading to it was her fault, a result of her angry lies.

Lew said: "Hello, Ira. Hello, Guy."

They didn't reply. They just glowered at him. At last Ira said: "You still here?"

"I'm here." Lew smiled faintly.

Ira sneered. "You're not *going* to have the gall to be at Max's funeral, are you?"

Lew saw Leona flinch. He shook his head. "As a matter of fact, I'm not. I've got something else to do."

There was an uneasy silence in the room. Lew stared at Ira steadily and watched the man's glance fall away. He said: "You drew up that lease for Gib, didn't you?"

"What if I did?"

"You know it's illegal."

Ira glanced at him mockingly. "Is it?"

"Yes. And I'm not going to honor it."

Ira glanced at Leona. He said: "Maybe you're not going to have a damn' thing to say about it."

Lew's glance flicked to Leona. Her eyes were downcast, and she didn't speak. Lew said: "You never give up, do you, Ira?"

Lew supposed Ira had been talking to Leona. He'd bullied her into agreeing to withdraw her support from Lew. Probably it hadn't taken too much persuasion. She was shocked and unnerved and filled with guilt. Probably at this point she wanted peace, no matter what it cost. Besides, she had no reason to be fond of Lew. She might still hate him for what had happened the other night. No woman likes to be refused, particularly when she has made her offer so plain it cannot be misunderstood.

Lew said: "What about it, Leona?"

She didn't get a chance to answer. From outside in the courtyard Lew heard his name being shouted. There was the sound of many hoofs, the good-natured bantering of many voices. The crew was ready.

Ira looked puzzled. Guy scowled. Ira said: "What the hell is this?"

"We're going to kick your god-damned leaseholder off Forty-Five."

"Oh, no, you're not!"

Lew grinned mockingly. "Try and stop us."

Ira strode swiftly to the door, with Guy at his heels. He burst out onto the gallery. His face was white with rage. He bellowed: "All of you! Put those horses away. You're not going any place."

All eyes switched uncertainly from Ira to Guy. Lew, standing behind Guy, could see that Guy was furious because Ira had given the order instead of deferring to him. His position as eldest in the family was one of which he was very jealous, probably because nobody else ever gave it much consideration. Belatedly he said: "Go on. Put your horses away. Max's funeral is today and any man that doesn't attend can hunt another job."

The men milled in the yard silently. Lew walked out to the horse Slim was leading, took the reins, and swung to the saddle. They watched him confusedly. "Let's go," he said.

Nobody moved. Slim looked straight at Lew, his face troubled and uneasy. He asked: "Lew, what the hell are we supposed to do? Who's givin' the orders around here anyway?"

Lew felt anger stirring in him. It showed in his eyes, in the tight set of his mouth.

Slim said aggrievedly: "Damn it, don't get mad at me. Guy and Ira are part owners of Forty-Five. You're not. Put yourself in our position."

Lew glanced at Ira and Guy. Both were smiling triumphantly. He swung back to the crew. He said: "I'm riding south to kick Roma off Forty-Five. If nobody goes with me, I'm going alone. The last I heard, I was running Forty-Five. Nobody's told me different. Now who's going and who's staying?"

More hesitation on the part of the crew. More uneasy glances, from Lew to Guy to Ira, and back again to Lew. Ira said: "Last you heard you were in charge. Well, that's changed. Leona says you're not in charge."

Lew said evenly: "I'll hear that from her."

Ira chuckled nastily. "All right. Hear it from her." He raised his voice. "Leona!"

She came to the open door behind him. Listlessly she stepped out onto the gallery. She refused to look at Lew, or meet his eyes.

Ira said: "Tell him. Tell him who's running Forty-Five."

Lew said: "Before you do, Leona, think a minute. Ira and Guy are going to let Roma stay just to get even with me. But Roma won't be satisfied with that. He'll push and crowd until he's living in this house instead of you. He's a killer, Leona. Do you think J.W. would want Mike's killer living on Forty-Five?"

He didn't like to bring J.W. into the discussion, but he was fighting now for the life of .45.

Leona glanced at him piteously. She seemed to be looking beyond his anger, searching his very soul. Then she faced the crew. "Lew is in charge." She turned and fled into the house.

Ira bawled: "Oh, no, he's not! Any man that rides with Lew today can draw his time! Who the hell do you think pays the wages around here? Lew? Not by a long shot. Go with Lew today, and when you get back, you'll find your gear lying outside on the ground."

Lew glanced around at the faces of the crew. In every face he saw anger, confusion, resentment at the position in which they had been placed. In spite of his desperate anxiety, he felt a certain sympathy for them. They weren't hired to take sides in a family conflict. It was unfair to demand it of them. But Lew had no choice. He had to demand it. And he couldn't afford to show his sympathy. If he did, it would be tantamount to relaxing his demand that they accompany him. He said: "Come on. Let's go. Every damned one of you!"

He turned and rode toward the gate. Behind him, he could hear Ira and Guy, both shouting at once. Their voices were a shrill babel of confusion. He heard another sound as well—the resentful grumbling of members of the crew. But he didn't look around. He rode straight to the gate. Only when he was clear of the gates did he look around. Four men were with him. The others had remained behind. Slim Clark and his shadow, stumpy Jess Leonard, ranged up beside him. The oldster, Dad Lloyd, and the kid, Sonny Rose, made up the remainder of the four-some.

Lloyd was scowling. Sonny Rose was scared. He looked around wistfully, as though he'd like to turn and gallop back. Slim said: "Can we do it with five?"

Lew nodded. They'd do it with five, all right. They had no choice.

XVII

Even though he had four of .45's crew riding with him, Lew could not help but feel a sting of failure. Five just wasn't enough. It wasn't enough to handle Roma's crew, which surely must consist of twelve to fifteen men. It wasn't enough to round up Roma's cattle. It wasn't enough to do anything. The best Lew could hope for was to inflict heavy casualties in a surprise attack. Or to get Roma himself and thus take the backbone out of his crew's resistance.

Furthermore, he could sense regret in the men who rode with him. Loyalty to Lew and to J.W. had dictated their joining him, not common sense. Now they were beginning to wonder just how foolish they had been, and what the price of their foolishness was going to be.

He looked at Slim and grinned. "Want to back out?"

Slim colored. "No, by God," he blustered. "Damn if that ain't a hell of a question to ask a man!"

Lew looked at Jess Leonard, at Lloyd and Sonny Rose in turn. "How about you? Peel off here if you want. No hard feelings if you do."

All of them looked sheepish. All stubbornly shook their heads.

Lew said: "This is going to be tough. Roma must have at least twelve or fifteen men."

Nobody replied. At last Slim Clark said: "Maybe we were thinkin' about quittin' on you but that don't mean we really would've done it. I been on Forty-Five for fifteen years. It's home. If I got to get planted here, then, by God, it's all right. I wouldn't want to be planted no place else."

These honest words warmed Lew, but he had not yet satisfied his conscience. He looked at Dad Lloyd and at Sonny Rose. Rose's thin face was twitching slightly and his sharp, pointed nose was running. Lew said: "You weren't hired on to fight . . . not odds like this, at least."

Lloyd said harshly: "You talk too much. A man hires on for the good and the bad both. Now let's get going. Let's get these god-damn' squatters moved off Forty-Five before they put down roots."

Lew thanked Lloyd with his eyes. He turned, and touched

the spurs to his horse's sides. They rode on south.

Slowly the sun climbed up the sky. Slowly the miles rolled behind. Off to his left, Lew could see Buffalo Hump rising above the plain, and remembered J.W. He was glad the old man wasn't here to see the bickering and hatred his death had generated.

At noon they stopped, watered their horses at a seep, and again rode on. At 1:00, they began seeing Roma's scrawny, wild-eyed Texas cattle. At 2:00, Lew called a halt.

In a dry arroyo they dismounted. Slim Clark asked: "Where you reckon they are?"

Lew frowned. He had been wondering the same thing himself. He said: "They'd want a place they could defend. They wouldn't know we'd have trouble getting enough men. I figure the badlands, maybe on that high hill about a mile inside, or over at Castle Rock."

The others talked it over a few moments, and Lew listened. Clark said: "I'll put my money on Castle Rock. For one thing, there's water right at the foot of it and plenty of horse feed on its slopes. Over in the badlands there ain't a damn' thing, either water or grass."

Lew nodded. "That's what I figured. So it's Castle Rock. But not right now. They could see us coming five miles away." He stopped, then ordered: "Lloyd, you and Sonny ride a scout into the badlands. Make sure they aren't there. Then come back here."

Lloyd and Sonny Rose rode off. Lew lay down on the floor of the arroyo in the shade. He stared up at the sky. Then, surprisingly, he went to sleep.

It seemed as though he had slept only a moment, but when he awakened, the sun was more than an hour lower in the sky. Slim Clark was shaking his shoulder. "Wake up, Lew. There's somebody hightailin' it toward Castle Rock."

Lew got up and followed Clark out of the arroyo. They walked up to the top of a low hill and stared west toward the towering, flat-topped butte called Castle Rock. Slim pointed.

Squinting, Lew made out a trail of dust. It seemed to be following a course between .45 and Castle Rock. He breathed: "Guy. Or Ira. God damn them, they've been working with Roma, or they wouldn't know where he was."

Slim said: "Maybe they're guessing, just like we did."

"Maybe." But Lew didn't believe it. Guy and Ira wouldn't hesitate to side with .45's enemies in order to dislodge Lew. They hated him that much.

For an instant, he wondered if it was worth it, fighting to hold something together that nobody else really cared about. Then his jaw hardened. J.W. had built it. J.W. would want it held together. And, by God, Lew was going to hold it together! Slim murmured: "There goes our surprise."

Lew nodded. Whoever that rider was, he had destroyed what little chance Lew had of bringing this off successfully. Roma would soon know that Lew had only four men.

He squinted, studying the lay of the land between here and Castle Rock. Arroyos cut it up, mostly running toward Castle Rock and the rising country behind it. They just might be able to work their way along these arroyos without showing themselves more than once or twice. If they could get in close before Roma got set. . . .

Forted up in an arroyo, they might still be able to do some good. Roma's knowledge of their numbers might be turned to their advantage. He might be tricked into attacking them.

Lew turned and outlined his plan to Slim. "If we can get in close before dark and open up, maybe Roma will attack. If he does, we'll hurt him as bad as we can, then hightail it out of there as soon as it gets dark."

Slim nodded. "Too bad you sent Lloyd and Sonny into the badlands."

"They ought to be back pretty soon. We'll have to wait."

He and Slim returned to the arroyo. Lew made a smoke and lit it, tossed the sack to Slim, who tossed it on to Jess. Lew smoked nervously. They waited. The sun dropped lower and lower toward the western horizon.

At last, near 4:30, Lloyd and Sonny Rose returned. "Not in the badlands, Lew," reported Lloyd.

Lew got up and caught his horse. He swung to the saddle and the others followed suit. He headed out, following the arroyo west.

It followed a crooked, tortuous path, but it brought them inexorably nearer to Castle Rock. Three miles from the place where they had started, it petered out and they had to find another. Leading his horse, Lew went first, and the others followed, one by one. There was a chance they would be seen, but it was a chance they'd have to take. If they were seen, Roma would simply lay an ambush for them at a bend in the arroyo they were following. They'd never know he was waiting until they rode into it.

Tension built steadily in Lew, but he didn't slow and he didn't stop. Three times they had to leave the arroyo they were following. Three times they found another. And at last, just as the sun sank behind the ponderous, rock-rimmed peak, Lew drew his horse to a halt. "Close enough," he said.

He swung down, pulling his rifle from the boot. He said: "Sonny, hold the horses."

Sonny looked at him glumly, but he took the horse's reins without protest. Lew climbed the precipitous side of the arroyo until he could see over the top.

Near the top of Castle Rock, the rimrock was gashed by erosion. Below that spot, boulders were tumbled around like a child's toy blocks. In this jumble of rock, Lew caught the movement of a horse. He said: "They're there, all right."

Slim squinted. "Five or six hundred yards at least. And uphill. Not much chance of hitting anything at that range."

Lew grinned. "We don't care if we hit them or not. All we want to do is smoke them out. A dozen shots ought to do the trick."

He found himself a comfortable spot where he could shoot while partially protected by the arroyo's bank. The others did likewise.

Lew laid his rifle on the bank. He sighted carefully on a horse's rump that showed behind one of the boulders. Then he lifted his rifle until his point of aim was almost a yard above the horse. He thumbed back the hammer and squeezed the trigger.

The sound of the shot was startling in the still air. It echoed and reëchoed from the rimrock above. Even at this distance Lew heard the bullet strike the rock beside the horse. The horse disappeared in a lunging jump.

Immediately the rifles of the three with him barked spitefully. Up on the peak, a man howled either with pain or surprise.

For an instant there was only silence. Then smoke began to puff from rifle muzzles up there, bullets began to kick up dust in front of the arroyo in which the four men lay. Lew grinned. A bullet struck two or three feet in front of him and showered dirt into his face. He ducked instinctively, then poked his head back up.

He fired at a puff of muzzle smoke. Next to him, the others were firing spasmodically.

Lew said: "All right. That's enough. Reload, all of you."

The firing stopped. Lew shoved bullets into his Winchester until the magazine was full. He said: "Give 'em a chance to think that over for a while."

He saw three horses file up through the cleft in the rimrock, their riders crouching low in their saddles. He said: "Three horsemen heading out behind the peak to flank us." He waited, wondering how smart he had been, knowing those three, and possibly others, would be working up behind him inside of twenty minutes. When they were in position, the main group would come charging down the slope to attack them from the front. Pinched between two groups, they wouldn't have a chance.

But if the main group could be lured into attacking *before* the others had worked their way up from the rear. . . . His grin widened. He said: "Slim, go tie the horses. Take Sonny and work your way down this arroyo for a couple of hundred yards. When you hear me shoot, open up in this direction. Make it look like there are more than two of you if you can. We'll be firing in your direction, but don't pay any attention to it. When you see that bunch come charging down off the mountain, hotfoot it back here and help us out."

Slim nodded admiringly. He slid down the bank and disappeared.

Lew waited. When he guessed ten minutes had passed, he rolled on his back and fired in the direction Slim had gone. Lloyd and Jess Leonard joined him enthusiastically. Immediately their fire was returned by Slim and Sonny Rose.

Lew stopped firing and glanced over his shoulder. He could see men mounting up behind the rocks on the peak. He heard a faint yell, and a few moments later eight horsemen came charging down the steep side of the peak, fanning out in a long line.

The firing beside Lew stopped, and he cautioned quickly: "Keep it up. Keep it up until they're halfway down."

That took but a few brief moments. He could hear Slim and Sonny Rose running along the floor of the arroyo. They arrived an instant later and, panting, eluded the bank.

Lew said: "Nice work. We smoked them out. They think their

own bunch is behind us, giving us hell. Let's show 'em how wrong they are."

He lined his sights on a galloping horseman, then led a bit and squeezed off his shot. The horse somersaulted down the slope, throwing his rider thirty feet. The man didn't move after he stopped rolling, but the horse got up and limped away.

In rapid succession, three more men were knocked out of their saddles. The remaining four veered away and galloped out of sight behind the edge of the hill.

Lew said: "All right. Get your horses. Fast!"

He scrambled down the slope after his men. They mounted quickly and, led by Lew, thundered along the arroyo toward the left side of the peak.

As soon as he could, Lew pulled his horse up out of it, onto the rolling plain. Wheeling left, he galloped hard for about a mile, the others close behind. Then, sighting dust rising from the arroyo they had just left, he turned again and galloped to its edge.

Riding there, he saw below him the three Roma had sent out to flank him from the rear. They stared up at him in surprise. Yanking out his Colt, he shot and missed. Slim shot one of the men in the shoulder, tumbling him from the saddle. The others' shots went wild.

Lew reined away before a bullet had been fired in their direction. He pounded hard toward the south, hoping they could lose themselves in the badlands before Roma could recover and pursue. They had downed four on the slope of Castle Rock, another in the arroyo. Of the five, only four, he guessed, were permanently out of the fight. Roma must still have eight or ten men. And he wouldn't be taken in so easily again.

Followed by his men, Lew rode steadily and very hard for more than half an hour. Then, cresting a rise, he glanced behind.

They were already lined out on his trail. From the looks of

their dust, he judged they were coming fast. He tried to count them, and thought he counted eight, but he could not be sure. Probably Roma had left at least one behind to help the wounded.

His mouth was a grim, straight line. In spite of the lack of surprise, they had come off well in the initial encounter. But the next time would be different. Roma's men would be on guard. They would be content with cautious sniping, and would make no headlong charges.

They were crossing a wide flat just at the edge of the badlands when Jess Leonard's horse put his foot in a prairie-dog hole. The horse went down, throwing Leonard clear. Lew reined up, plunging, and swung back. Leonard got up and limped toward him at a shambling run.

Lew gave him a stirrup and Leonard swung up behind, hitting the horse's rump behind the saddle with a solid thump. Lew drew his gun and shot Leonard's horse, which was struggling to get up in spite of a broken leg. Then he reined around and pounded along in the wake of the other three.

He hadn't counted on this. Riding double would slow them down. And there was still more than two hours of daylight left. And now, Roma's eight began to overhaul Lew and his four, steadily and inexorably. At the end of half an hour, the pursuers were less than a mile behind.

Lew plunged recklessly into the badlands. In minutes he was out of sight of the pursuers, but it gave him no false sense of security. He knew the badlands better than they possibly could. He also knew that chance played an important part in the chase now. If Roma slavishly followed trail, they were safe. If Roma tried to anticipate Lew's movements, there was a possibility he could get ahead of Lew.

Circling, backtracking, riding with complete disregard for personal safety, Lew worked slowly deeper into the badlands. And he began to work eastward, preparatory to leaving the badlands and coming out again onto the grassy plain. The light faded. All four horses were lathered and steaming. Lew's, carrying double, was breathing harshly, his lungs a giant, laboring bellows.

At last, Lew knew they had to stop. They had to stop or lose another horse.

He drew rein behind an eroded, red clay butte. He waited until Jess Leonard swung down, then swung down himself. He unbuckled the cinch and lifted the saddle off. He began to fan the horse with the sodden saddle blanket.

The others had their saddles off, too, and were following Lew's example. The faces of Slim and Sonny Rose were confident, smiling. Lloyd was frowning. Older than the others, he knew this badlands country better than they. He knew how the cañons had a way of interlocking, of running into each other. He knew how good was the chance that Roma and his men would stumble on their quarry by pure accident. He said softly to Lew: "We've lost 'em for now. How soon you figuring to get out of here?"

"Right now. As soon as the horses are rested."

He paced back and forth nervously. Most of the light had gone from the sky. The sun was well down, but its dying rays touched a few high clouds with pink. Except for that, the sky was a deep, cold gray. Lew thought: *Another fifteen minutes. Another fifteen minutes and we'll be safe.*

He had scarcely finished the thought when he heard a clatter of hoofs, too close, and saw Roma and his men sweep around a bend in the dry-wash floor. Damn the way sound was muffled by this soft, dry sand! He yanked out his revolver and snapped a shot at the milling crowd.

They were as surprised as he, as startled. They hauled their horses in, rearing, and scattered like quail to right and left. Lew yelled: "Slim! Jess! Sonny! Saddle up! Dad and I will cover you!"

He dived behind a rock. His first shot caught one of Roma's men in the calf of the leg and the man went down, sprawling. He crawled behind a rock, and Lew let him go, content to shower the man with rock splinters as he scrambled to safety.

Behind him, he heard the frantic movements of Jess and Sonny and Slim as they tried to saddle up. Haste was against them, for it made their fingers fumble, and frightened the horses.

Lew snapped a shot at a man with a rifle just as the rifle boomed. He heard Sonny Rose yell with pain, and, swinging his head, saw Sonny clutch an arm, his face white and shocked.

Dad Lloyd stood up, scorning cover, and laid a withering fire among the rocks behind which the attackers were hidden. Lew saw their heads go down. He yelled: "Damn it, Dad, get down!"

Slim shouted: "All ready, Lew!"

Lew swung his head momentarily. "All right. You and Jess take Sonny. Get the hell out of here. We'll cover you."

It was almost dark. Another five minutes—ten. . . .

Lew swung back, his revolver reloaded, and began to fire. There wasn't much in the way of targets—a head here, a rifle barrel or part of an arm there. And the light was bad.

He heard the bullet that struck Dad Lloyd as Slim and Jess thundered away on their horses. He hadn't time to look. He fired frantically at muzzle flashes, praying he could spoil the shooters' aim until Jess and Slim could get away with Sonny Rose.

The hoof beats faded. Lew lunged to his feet and ran toward the place where Lloyd lay. A bullet tore through his left shoulder. He flung himself down and slid the last three feet to where Lloyd lay behind a rock.

He could scarcely see Lloyd's face. He put a hand on Lloyd's chest. There was no rise and fall of breathing. He moved his hand so that it lay directly over Lloyd's heart. There was no movement, no steady beat. Lloyd was dead.

Fury rose in Lew, aggravated by the shock of his wound, by the growing pain. But he did not let it affect his reason. He stripped Dad's cartridge belt off and buckled it around his own waist. His arm was growing numb.

Quickly he went through Dad's pockets for rifle cartridges. He found a couple dozen and stuffed them into his own pockets. They were of the same caliber as his own. Next, he pulled a clean bandanna from his hip pocket and rolled up his sleeve. It was completely dark now and he couldn't see the wound. Warm blood was running down his arm, and he knew it was bad. He laid a hand over the wound, trying to tell by feel if the blood was spurting or coming in a steady flow. If it was spurting, he'd be dead in half an hour.

He thought it was only a steady flow, and so, awkwardly, he tied it, using his teeth to pull one end of the knot, his good hand the other. All was quiet now. All was deathly still save for an occasional sound from one of the horses as he fidgeted or moved away.

Lew raised his head and fired three times at random, left, center, and right. Instantly half a dozen guns flared and the bullets slammed into the rock before him. Lew raised up and fired two more times. Then, holding the gun between his body and left elbow, he reloaded awkwardly with his right hand.

His head was reeling. He felt that if he stood up, he would totter and fall. He wondered if this was to be the end for him. Then anger stirred again. To hell with that! He'd done his best, and it hadn't been good enough. But he wasn't through. He wasn't through yet!

He fired again, several random shots, then when the answering muzzle flares showed, he emptied his gun at them. He was rewarded by a sharp intake of breath and a groan of pain. Grinning savagely, he began to inch back toward the horses. Before he reached them, he stood up and walked the last few yards.

He tied up the reins of his own exhausted horse. Then he mounted the other. His left arm dangled uselessly now, completely numb. Holding the reins of his own mount in his teeth, he cut the loose horse viciously across the rump with the sight of his revolver.

The animal thundered away, straight toward Roma and his men. Their guns opened up instantly, and Lew could hear the sodden sound of bullets striking the horse's flesh. He heard the horse go down, heard the animal's frantic thrashing afterward. Then he was riding away, slowly, quietly, so as not to make a sound that would be audible over the uproar behind him.

They'd discover their error soon enough. But by the time they did, Lew hoped to be a quarter mile away, lost in the inky dark.

XVIII

As soon as the shouts of the men behind him died in his ears, Lew touched spurs to his horse's sides. He headed straight out of the badlands, knowing he had to have help, and soon, if he was going to live. He rode steadily for half an hour, without hearing sounds of pursuit behind him, knowing well that lack of sound didn't mean a thing. They could be less than a quarter mile away.

A glow in the east drew his eyes, and for a moment his pain-drugged mind was puzzled. It looked like a monstrous fire blazing just below the horizon. He watched it for a moment, then the awful truth burst upon him. It was the moon, nearly full, rising in the east. Another fifteen minutes and the plain would be bathed with light. As full as it was and as bright, it would provide enough light for Roma to follow his trail. He had to keep riding. He couldn't stop. If he stopped, they'd follow his trail and kill him before midnight.

He lined the horse out in a northerly direction and, gritting his teeth against the growing pain in his arm and shoulder, spurred him to a lope. He could not count on receiving help from Slim and Jess. Riding double, carrying a wounded man, they would be intent only on escape. And it was doubtful if, upon reaching Medicine Lodge, they'd be able to persuade anyone to render help to Lew himself. The sheriff was solidly on the side of the Regals and the Regals were solidly supporting Roma.

He rode steadily. The moon came up, forcing him to cling to the western slope, to gullies and arroyos, to avoid being outlined by its clear, cold light.

An hour passed. Two. Behind him he heard a distant shout.

Panic touched him. He felt like a hunted animal. He felt the rise of a cornered animal's fury within him. Damn Roma! Damn him to hell! He must have eyes like a hawk to be able to trail this fast by moonlight.

Lew cursed the chance that made it necessary for him to cling to shadows as he rode. He scanned the skies for clouds. There were a few, but they drifted maddeningly along, well away from the moon. His dizziness mounted. His head felt light, and his body seemed almost to be floating. He was conscious of only two things—the terrible pain in his arm and shoulder, and the hunters behind him.

He heard their shouts often now, and knew they were gaining. He forced clarity to his thoughts with a determined effort of will. Where was he going? Where would he find shelter and safety? At .45? He shook his head. At Santoyo's shack? That was the first place they'd look for him.

His thoughts fuzzed again. He was but barely conscious now. He clung desperately to the saddle horn, not even guiding his horse. His head dropped. And then, out of his long-dead childhood came the solution. There was a place about three miles from Santoyo's shack. As a boy, Lew had dug out the bank of a low bluff beneath a huge, flat, buried rock. He had made a little cave there where he used to go when he was playing mountain man and was trying to evade a bunch of imaginary Cheyennes. He hadn't seen it for years, but the last time he had he'd noticed that brush had grown up heavily in front of it, enough to screen it almost completely.

He raised his head with an effort. He looked around him for landmarks, trying to orient himself. Then he turned his horse. Two miles. Two miles to go. If he could last that long. . . .

He did. He reached the place still conscious. And now he dismounted, looking up at it. What to do with the horse and saddle? If he tied the reins up, the horse would return to .45. And if he did that, it would be a simple matter to track him here in the morning. Lew shook his head angrily to clear it. Then he decisively stripped bridle and saddle from the horse and gave him a cut across the rump. The horse trotted away.

Lew watched him go, gathering strength to lug the heavy saddle, the rifle, and two holstered revolvers up the hill. The horse would wander, aimlessly perhaps, until he found some other horses. But even if he was found tomorrow, it would be a virtual impossibility to track him back to this place.

Lew knew he mustn't make any trail from here to the cave. If he did, he was sunk. Cautiously he slung the saddle to his shoulder. The left arm dangled uselessly, without strength and without feeling. He stepped carefully up the hill, staying to grass clumps that, he hoped, would spring back up again before morning.

He thought he would never reach it, but he refused to stop until he did. He slung his saddle in, no longer able to care about the crash it made breaking through the brush that screened the opening. He crawled after it groggily. He sprawled inside, taking time only to remove the rifle from the scabbard on the saddle and lay it beside him. Then, resting his head on the saddle, he sighed deeply and lost consciousness.

He didn't know how long he had slept, but it was still dark when he awoke. Turning his head, he could see the moonlight outside through the screen of brush. His shoulder and arm were afire with pain, and it occurred to him that he might have groaned in his sleep.

Closing his hand on the rifle, he eased around until he was facing the opening. He peered out cautiously. Below him in the draw were several horses and men, and he knew instantly that they had awakened him.

Two of them were dismounted, and following trail. Lew eased the rifle against his body to muffle the sound of the action and cautiously levered a shell into the chamber. He waited.

The two on the ground halted and conferred in low tones for a moment or two. Then one of them turned and called: "Frenchy, send someone to town for the sheriff. Tell him that damned Stark killed two of my men. Tell him I've got a legitimate lease and I want him to find Stark and jail him for murder."

He heard another man issuing orders, and a moment later one of the mounted men galloped away toward town. They hadn't found his trail then. Not yet. But if they stayed down there much longer, they were sure to find it.

With one hand, he eased the rifle awkwardly to his shoulder. He sighted on the larger of the two men on the ground, knowing he was Roma. If they found Lew's trail, Roma would die before he discovered which way it led. Lew promised himself that.

The rifle muzzle steadied on Roma's chest. Lew's finger tightened around the trigger. The smaller man with Roma said:

"Here's the trail."

He wandered off slowly down the arroyo, and the others followed. Lew released a long, soft sigh of relief. Good thing he'd awakened when he had. Sound carried well on this clear night air, and one soft groan would have given him away.

A good thing, too, that they were trailing by moonlight and not by the clear light of the sun. Otherwise, that tracker would have known that from here on, the horse he followed was riderless.

Lew turned and laboriously dragged the saddle to the opening so that he could rest his head on it and still face the outside. He closed his eyes. Waves of nausea and pain washed through him. He wondered if he would die here without ever getting out, and lie unfound until the flesh rotted from his bones. His situation was even worse now than it had been before. Hearing but one side of the argument, badgered by Roma and the two Regal brothers, Joe Riker would have little choice. He'd have to issue a warrant for Lew, charging him with murder. And that would be exactly what Roma and the Regals wanted. It would, in effect, give them a hunting license legalizing the killing of Lew wherever and whenever they found him. Lew's consciousness faded.

When he woke again, it was light, and the sun was high in the sky. The heat inside this little cave was increasing, and Lew knew that as the sun traveled westward and beat against the mouth of the cave, it would become unbearable. Already his mouth and throat were dry and cracked. Already delirium reached for him.

He moved, and the pain in his arm brought a stifled shout to his lips. He edged closer to the mouth of the cave, pulled aside a clump of brush, and peered outside. Over there was Buffalo Hump. To his right and half a mile away was Comanche Springs.

Water. But it might as well have been a thousand miles away.

The sun moved slowly toward the west. Lew lost consciousness and regained it, and lost it again. His reason faded, and he shouted with delirium. And then, in one of his brief periods of lucid awareness, he saw a single rider coming toward him across the endless grass.

His vision blurred, but he raised the rifle and sighted carefully. The rider came on, as though he knew of the cave, as though he knew exactly where he was going. Lew's finger tightened on the trigger. The muzzle wavered, and he couldn't steady it to save his life.

The rider dismounted at the foot of the slope. Tying the horse to a clump of brush, he began to climb. Lew steadied his gun as best he could and pulled the trigger. The gun roared and smoke belched from its muzzle. The recoil caused a blinding pain in Lew's shoulder. He blinked his eyes, and all he could see were whirling spots. He pointed the gun aimlessly, levered in a shell, and pulled the trigger. Maybe they had him treed, but it was going to cost them to get him down.

And then he heard a voice, crying out. "Lew! Lew! Stop shooting. It's me!"

Fear struck him. He crawled to the cave opening and frantically clawed aside the brush. He saw her coming, almost running up the slope. She seemed to be unhurt.

Then she was at the cave opening and crawling inside. He seized the canteen she carried and twisted off the cap. He poured water into his mouth, choked on it, and began to cough. Water ran down the sides of his mouth and onto his filthy, blood-soaked shirt.

When he could, he gasped hoarsely: "How'd you find me, Nata? How'd you know?"

"This is the only place for a dozen miles that a man could hide. I knew you were either dead, or hiding here."

She pushed him back and held the canteen to his mouth. This time he drank more slowly. Then she opened a pocket knife and began to cut his shirt away from his wound. As she worked, she talked softly in Spanish. There was an outraged virulence in her voice and occasionally he recognized a Spanish curse.

When she had cleansed the wound with water, when she had loosened the shirt that had stuck to it, she got up and left the cave. She went down the slope to her horse and there got salves and bandages for it.

Lew looked down at the wound, fighting to retain consciousness. There was a small, bluish hole in front. In back, where the bullet had come out, there was a ragged, shredded hole as big as a silver dollar. It oozed blood that ran down his back. But the bullet hadn't hit a bone. And, barring infection, it would heal.

Natalia returned, looked at his face, and said: "Lew, for heaven's sake, lie down before you fall down."

Lew let her ease him back onto the saddle. Her face blurred before him. Natalia began to bandage his wound. Everything went black.

For an hour after she had finished, Natalia Santoyo sat cross-legged beside him, her eyes resting gently on his face. He needed a doctor, and a bed. He needed quiet until his wound had time to heal. But Natalia was a realist. She knew there was no place Lew could go. There was no safety for him any place but here.

Natalia was small, and a woman besides. But as she looked at Lew, an angry fierceness began to grow in her eyes. If there was no safe place for Lew, then someone must make a safe place for him. In the meantime, if he had water and food, he would be all right here.

Carefully, so as not to disturb him, she eased out of the cave. She ran down the slope to her horse, mounted, and rode away toward home.

Upon arriving, she unsaddled her horse and put him into the corral. She did not want anyone to know she had been gone. She went inside and built up the fire in the stove. Her eyes smoldered with anger. Her lovely mouth was set with quiet fury. She boiled some meat for soup, put on coffee. She got a couple of loaves of the bread she had baked yesterday, spread a couple of wool blankets on the floor, and laid the bread in the center of the blankets. The aroma of cooking meat and boiling coffee filled the room. Natalia paced restlessly back and forth, waiting.

Outside, she heard the distant drum of hoofs. Snatching up Mike's rifle, she jacked a cartridge into the chamber, and went to the door.

Roma swept into the yard at the head of half a dozen men. He looked at her briefly, contemptuously. He turned his head. "Dave, check that horse in the corral. See if he's hot."

A man detached himself from the others and rode toward the corral. Natalia swung the muzzle of the rifle and fired. Dust kicked up immediately in front of Dave French's horse. The animal reared.

Dave looked at Roma uncertainly. Roma's hand lay threateningly on the grips of his gun, but Natalia's gun muzzle covered him steadily. She said softly: "Get out of here. Now!"

Roma blustered. "Now you wait a minute! No damned Mexican bitch is going to tell me. . . ."

Natalia's gun bellowed. Roma's horse jumped under the impact of the bullet, then folded, front legs first, to the ground. Roma's face, as he stepped clear, was white with fury. But his hand dropped away from his gun.

Natalia said coldly: "Put a rope around his neck. Drag him out of my yard. And keep going."

Roma stared at her appraisingly for a moment. He turned his

head. "Do what she says!" He stayed there on the ground, looking at her, his eyes filled with deadly, baffled rage.

Two of his men dropped their loops onto the dead horse's head. One of the others got down and lifted it to slip the loops over it. The two men spurred away, their horses plunging against the dead weight of the downed horse. It slid slowly out of the yard.

They dragged it a couple hundred yards. One of them dismounted and removed the ropes, and the two came riding back.

Roma said furiously to Natalia: "I'm not through with you."

Natalia's glance didn't waver, though fear was a ball of ice against her spine. She said evenly: "The next bullet is going straight through your chest."

Roma turned, trying to maintain dignity and failing utterly. He climbed up behind Dave French, awkward because of his injured foot. He looked around, and his mouth opened to speak. Natalia raised the gun slightly and sighted along its barrel.

French's horse lunged as Roma dug spurs into his flanks. The animal plunged away, with Roma clinging to French, both arms locked around his body.

Natalia laughed. Her laughter was savagely mocking. Dull red suffused the back of Roma's neck. The six horses disappeared over a rise of ground.

Natalia went into the house and checked her soup. Then, still carrying the rifle, she went to the corral and saddled up. She rode out in the direction Roma and his men had gone.

She rode for several miles, without catching sight of them, without finding tracks of a single horse breaking off from the bunch. Satisfied that Roma had not detailed a man to spy on her, she returned to the shack.

She found a couple of half-gallon jam jars and carefully, so as not to break the glass, filled one with coffee and the other with soup. She put them on the blankets with the bread, added a cup and spoon, and wrapped the blankets around them. Carrying her bundle and rifle, she went out and mounted her horse.

She did not ride directly toward the cave. Instead, she headed out toward town. But when she had gone a mile, she climbed to a high point of land and scanned the surrounding country. Seeing nothing, she made a big circle a mile in diameter around her cabin, watching the ground for tracks. Satisfied at last, she headed straight for the cave. She was safe for now, and Lew was safe.

The let-down of tension crept insidiously over her. Her eyes, which had sparkled with anger and determination, now softened and filled with tears. Her lower lip quivered almost uncontrollably. Her body began to shake. She wept almost hysterically there on her horse for several minutes while he plodded stolidly toward the cave. Then, determinedly, she got hold of herself. She clenched her tiny fists and bit her lip until it bled. And by the time she reached the cave, her face was calm and determined again.

Lew awoke as she crawled into the cave, lugging her burden of blankets and food. She spooned hot soup from the jar into his mouth. She let him eat a little bread and drink a little coffee. She spread the blankets on the floor of the cave and helped him onto them. She covered him.

"I've got to go, Lew, but I'll be back. Don't stir from this cave except at night. Promise?"

He grinned at her weakly. There was a quality in his glance that repaid her fully for all she had done. She leaned down and kissed him on the mouth. Then she crawled out of the entrance to the cave. She mounted her horse and rode south, a tiny, straight-backed figure on a big, long-legged roan.

XIX

A mile from the Santoyo shack, Roma said savagely: "Get off this horse, French. Ride with one of the others."

French looked around angrily. He said nothing, but swung a leg over the horse's head, and slipped to the ground. Roma spurred away furiously, without waiting for the others.

When he heard them coming behind him, he slowed and let them catch up. Cold fury churned in him, made unbearable by his helplessness, by his defeat at the hands of that girl, a Mexican girl at that.

Where in the devil had that damned Lew Stark disappeared to? They'd trailed him all night, and Roma could have sworn that Chavez, his half-Indian tracker, hadn't lost the trail. But in the early morning, the tracks had blended with those of a band of loose horses, and had wandered aimlessly for several hours across the plain. Upon sighting the horses at dawn, Roma had given up.

Only Stark now stood in his way. Maybe there was a murder warrant out for him, but he had to be found before Roma could do anything about it. One thing was sure. Roma wasn't going to take Lew in. He was going to kill him the minute he saw him. And those Regal brothers. Roma's lips curled with contempt. Neither of them had the guts for Roma's kind of fight. Riding this huge ranch, Roma had felt a stir of envy. Hell, if he had a ranch like this. . . . Suddenly his eyes brightened. Why not? Why should he be satisfied with a lease when he could own the whole southern half of it? The brothers were in no position to defend their land. Their crew was scattered. What few remained were confused and dissatisfied. If Lew Stark were dead, there'd be nothing to stand in Roma's way. He could make things so precarious and miserable for the Regal bunch that they'd be glad to sell him the southern half of .45 for little or nothing just to get him off their backs.

Harassment of the Regals would be easy. Neither cared for ranch work or riding, and neither had the guts for fighting. If .45 cattle began to disappear into the badlands, if springs were poisoned, if buildings occasionally caught fire at .45. . . . He smiled. The Regals would come to terms. But not Lew Stark.

It always came back to that. Roma was afraid to move as long as Lew Stark lived. He remembered the savage, single-minded way Lew had of fighting. He remembered the look that had come into Lew's eyes as he'd fought that day in front of Santoyo's shack. No. He couldn't move until Lew Stark was dead. He had to find some way to smoke him out. . . .

Again his eyes brightened. There *was* a way. Then he shook his head. That was a kind of last resort, a plan to be used only if all else failed.

In the meantime, while he was hunting Lew, he might as well try and consolidate his hold on the southern half of .45. Maybe he could make a deal with the Regal brothers.

He reined his horse to a stop, and swung to look at French. "I want Lew Stark, and I want him dead. You and the others keep riding. One of you go back and keep an eye on Santoyo's place. I'll watch the home place at .45, because I'm going there. The rest of you keep looking. Keep Chavez looking for the trail. Stark's got to be here some place. If you don't find him by midnight, part of you come to .45, the others go to Santoyo's."

French nodded, a trifle surly, Roma thought. He turned and led the others away. Roma himself rode toward .45.

There were three members of .45's crew lounging before the bunkhouse. They looked at Roma impassively. He supposed this was all that was left of .45's crew. He was willing to bet that not a single man was out working, riding .45's vast miles of range.

He found Guy and Ira in the house. Roma looked at Guy and asked: "Did you get my men to town all right?"

Guy nodded, scowling. Ira asked eagerly, worriedly: "Did you get Lew?"

Roma shook his head, smiling inwardly with contempt. It was a good thing he'd come here now. This pair was waiting for him to get Lew Stark. When he had, they'd want no more to do with him. But he wasn't going to let it be that easy for them.

He said: "I've got cattle to take care of, and other things to do. If you expect me to get rid of Stark for you, you're going to have to make it worth my while."

They looked at him suspiciously. He saw fear behind the eyes of both, fear that he'd pull out and leave the problem of Lew Stark to them. Ira asked drily: "What do you want? What would it take to make it worth your while?"

Roma smiled bleakly. "This is too big a ranch for the two of you to run. That Mexican settlement south of the badlands will rob you blind. What you need is someone between you and the badlands to act as a buffer."

Comprehension began to dawn in Ira's eyes. Guy's scowl remained.

Roma said: "I want an option to buy fifty thousand acres off the southern end of Forty-Five at ten cents an acre. You can have the option expire in thirty days. If I haven't caught Stark by then, you can forget the whole damned thing."

"And if you do catch him?"

"I'll exercise my option."

Ira hesitated. His expression told Roma he knew how ridiculous the price was. It also told Roma how he feared Lew Stark. At last Ira said: "Leona owns half of Forty-Five."

Roma smiled. He had heard all about Leona Regal from the gossips in town. He said: "Leave Missus Regal to me."

Ira looked at Guy. "What do you think?"

Guy nodded, a crafty look in his eyes. Again contempt stirred in Roma. They'd give him an option, but they had no intention of honoring it. Ira clearly knew that an option signed only by the two of them would be worthless as the paper it was written on. Still, it would give Roma the appearance of legality, so far as the courts were concerned. It would give him justification for staying on .45 and holding it until the issue could be decided in the courts. By that time, he knew he could have both Regal brothers and Leona softened up. They'd be glad to sell. They'd do anything to get him off their backs.

He said: "All right, draw it up. I'll be back tomorrow for it. In the meantime, I'll hunt Lew Stark." He smiled at the pair confidently. "Until I find him, sit tight." He turned and went to the door. In the courtyard, he mounted, smiling grimly to himself. He could imagine what they were saying back there in the house. They thought they had outwitted him. Let them think it. It would lull their suspicions. The option would be ready tomorrow. After that. . . .

As he rode, Roma tried to put himself in Lew Stark's place. To whom would Stark turn? Roma knew he was wounded. Chavez had found traces of blood along the trail. Hell, there was no one to whom Stark *could* turn—except Natalia Santoyo and possibly Leona. Leona was out. Lew wouldn't dare show up at .45. So it had to be Natalia.

He turned his horse and headed for the Santoyo shack. He'd get that girl without her rifle and, by God, he'd *make* her talk.

It took him about an hour and a half to reach the place. When he did, he reined in atop a rise and looked the country over carefully. After a few moments he saw a figure standing on a far hill. The man waved his rifle over his head.

Roma circled and rode to him without exposing himself to the house. The sun was down now and dusk was creeping slowly across the sky. He reached the man, a slim twenty-five-year-old named Corbin. Roma asked: "Seen anything?"

Corbin shook his head. "The place looks deserted. She

must've turned her horse out of the corral. She ain't there now."

Roma walked carefully up the hill until he could see the San-toyo shack. Only his head was exposed to it. Frowning, he watched it for several minutes. Smoke drifted lazily from the chimney, but there was no other sign of life. The door was closed.

Roma felt a touch of concern. He said: "Ride on down there. See if she's there. If she is, talk to her. Get her outside if you can. I'll slip up behind the cabin. If she runs you off, leave. Don't argue with her."

"Don't worry, I won't." Corbin walked to his horse and mounted. He looked doubtfully at Roma. "I don't like this. Fightin' men is one thing. Fightin' women is another."

Roma looked at him coldly. "You want your time?"

The man fidgeted uneasily in his saddle. He mumbled—"Guess not."—and rode away. Roma walked back up the hill until he could see the shack.

He watched Corbin ride slowly down to it. Fifty feet from the door, Corbin reined up. He called: "Hello the house!"

Nothing happened. Corbin got down and walked hesitantly to the door. He knocked on it lightly. When there was no answer, he knocked harder. Still there was no answer.

He looked up the hill at Roma. He raised his hands, palms out in a gesture of helplessness.

Roma turned and went back to his horse. He mounted and spurred savagely over the hill and down to the bottom. Damn that wench! She'd got away. Probably as soon as they'd left, she'd flown the coop. He was willing to bet she was with Lew Stark right now.

When he reached the cabin, Roma dismounted and flung open the door. As he had suspected, the cabin was empty.

He turned furiously to Corbin. "You know where the others are? I want Chavez."

It was already too dark to see the ground, too dark to trail. Corbin said: "I think I can find 'em. They couldn't have got far in two, three hours."

Roma said savagely: "All right. Find 'em. I want Chavez here at dawn."

Corbin looked at him strangely. But he turned without a word, mounted and rode away.

Roma paced nervously back and forth before the cabin. Angrily then, he went inside. He built up the fire in the stove, found himself a side of bacon and a can of beans and fixed himself some supper. The coffee was still warm, and there was a big pan that held a little clear beef soup in its bottom—rations for a wounded man.

He bolted his food angrily. The more he thought of it the more furious he became. This place had unpleasant memories for him anyway. He looked down at the filthy, half-worn-out bandage on his foot. He didn't know whether it was healing or not. He supposed it was. The pain had been easing lately.

He went outside to the dirt-floored porch, glaring about him angrily. He saw the rusty axe head half buried in the ground. Suddenly his anger broke free of restraint. Almost running, he lunged into the house. He seized the edge of the stove and heaved it onto its side. The lids fell out and red-hot coals cascaded onto the floor.

Roma was like a maniac. He heaved chairs, tables, clothing, and anything else that was loose upon the growing fire. The room began to fill with smoke. Choking, coughing, at last he was forced to leave. He went outside, his eyes streaming tears, his face blackened and streaked with smoke. He stood there in the yard, watching while the flames mounted. And watching, he began to laugh.

Before morning, Chavez would be here. Roma would put him on the girl's trail. He'd find her, and he'd find Lew Stark.

Roma knew now that he'd find them together and when he did, by God, he'd kill them both.

XX

Lew Stark felt greatly strengthened by the soup, bread, and coffee that Natalia had brought him. He slept for a while after she left, then awoke and ate more of the soup, which was still warm. By the time he had finished, dusk was drifting across the land. Mindful of his promise to Natalia, however, he did not crawl outside until it was full dark.

The bluff in which the cave was situated faced west. He stood before it and fumbled automatically for tobacco and papers in his shirt pocket. He was surprised to find the sack still there, stuck to the inside of his pocket by the dried and crusted blood that had partially soaked it. He found an untouched paper in the center of the pack and shook tobacco into it. He shielded a match with his cupped hands and lit it. It was the first smoke he'd had in thirty-six hours and it tasted wonderfully good.

He had no idea where Natalia had gone. Probably to town to try and round up help for him. She'd have no luck. At this point Roma and the Regal brothers held all the cards. Everyone in Medicine Lodge would figure that Lew's was a lost cause.

He was weak from shock and loss of blood. His shoulder pained him, and was very stiff, but he was relieved to realize that the arm was no longer numb and without feeling. Staring out across the land, he saw a glow just above the horizon that reminded him of the one he'd seen while he was escaping from Roma and his men. That had been the moon, but this glow was in the northwest, in the direction of Santoyo's cabin, and could mean only one thing—Santoyo's place was burning.

Suddenly Lew forgot his weakness, forgot everything but the terrible anger that flooded him. This was senseless vindictiveness on Roma's part. Natalia Santoyo was no threat to his plans.

Besides, his war was with Lew and .45, not with a helpless girl.

Lew turned decisively. Crawling into the cave, he found the rifle. He strapped his revolver and cartridge belt around his middle. Then he went back outside.

He walked down the slope, surprised at the way his strength had returned. It was three miles to Santoyo's place. A long walk for Lew in his weakened condition. He'd be too late to save anything. But he would not be too late to find the one who was responsible. He promised himself that.

He walked swiftly, sure in his knowledge of the land. As he walked, the moon rose in the east, and the glow toward which he walked died and disappeared. When he crested the rise that looked into Santoyo's yard, the moon was well up in the sky behind him.

The cabin was a glowing heap of embers. He could see the outline of the stove lying on its side, glowing red-hot. He let his eyes rove over the yard and saw a horse standing tied to Mike Santoyo's buckboard about a hundred yards from the house.

There was an odd tightness to Lew's scalp, a strange crawling feeling in his brain. His vision fuzzed a little, then cleared again. Was this weakness from the wound, or was it something else? Could it be that his father had felt this way just before the killing for which he had been outlawed? One thing Lew knew— one thing only—that he wanted to kill Roma. He wanted to kill Roma more than he wanted any other thing.

Slowly he walked down the slope, which was partially in shadow. As it leveled out near the bottom, he crouched, remaining in the shadow. He was forced to crawl the last hundred feet in order to do so.

Motionless, he searched the moonlit yard with his eyes. Between himself and the tied horse, he saw a lumped shape upon the ground that he judged was a sleeping man. The brazenness of it astounded him. Roma must be very confident if he'd burn a cabin and then calmly go to sleep beside it. Lew grinned savagely. Roma's confidence was about to be shattered.

He glanced up at the sky, noting that a cloud layer was slowly drifting toward the moon. He'd have to wait. If Roma saw him, the man could reach his horse and escape. Moonlight shooting, even at a range of under a hundred yards, was a risky thing. And Lew did not want Roma to escape.

He decided to wait until the clouds obscured the moon. Then he'd move cautiously around until he was between Roma and his horse. He'd wait until the moon came out again. Then Roma would waken and die.

Accordingly, when the moon drifted behind the lazily moving clouds, Lew slipped along the side of the slope. He moved silently, like an Apache, testing each step before putting his weight down.

Over there on the ground, the man moved uncomfortably, turning in his blankets. Perhaps this wasn't Roma. Perhaps it was one of his men. But whoever it was, he had a debt to pay.

The horse fidgeted nervously as he caught Lew's scent. He drew away to the limit of his bridle reins, his ears laid back. Lew smiled grimly. The man on the ground hadn't even had the decency and consideration to picket his horse so that the animal could graze. He hoped the horse wouldn't snort or break away. But it was a chance he had to take.

Slowly, step by step, he drew nearer the horse. At last he stood within arm's reach. He put out a soothing hand and laid it on the horse's neck.

He could feel the animal flinch under his hand. But once contact had been made, the horse quieted.

Now Lew moved toward the sleeping man. The clouds had thickened over the moon and the only light in the yard was that cast by the embers of the smoldering cabin.

Lew glanced at the sky. Damn! Those clouds were here to

stay. He'd have to do this in the dark.

Slowly, carefully he moved toward the inert shape on the ground, testing each step as he went. And then, the unexpected, the almost impossible happened. Lew's toe touched an empty rusted lard pail, and it rolled away, rattling on the hard, dry ground.

Instantly the shape on the ground moved. Like a cat, the man sprang away, shedding blankets as he did. His gun flared, and Lew raised his rifle and fired at the flare. Then there was the sound of running feet, and the man disappeared into the darkness.

For an instant Lew was motionless. Desperately he wanted to pursue. Reason told him it was foolish. In this utter darkness the man could pass half a dozen yards away and not be seen. He could slip past Lew, reach his horse, and escape cleanly.

One other alternative occurred to Lew. He could go back and wait beside the horse. Sooner or later the man would come to him. Or would he? Wouldn't it pay him better simply to conceal himself and wait for dawn? By so doing he could pick Lew off in its first cold light with no risk whatsoever to himself.

Lew shook his head angrily. However he hated doing so, he would have to postpone his reckoning with Roma. He would have to take the horse and go.

With his mind made up, he retreated swiftly and silently to the horse. He untied the animal's reins awkwardly with his good hand, then swung swiftly astride.

Off in the darkness, a gun flared. Lew held his fire. He turned the horse and spurred away.

And now there was another decision to be made. Should he return to the cave like a rabbit to its burrow and hide? He shook his head. No. He belonged at .45. Whatever happened, he belonged at .45. Accordingly he turned the horse and rode that way.

An hour of riding lay ahead. But he could count on his arrival coming as a surprise. The man at Santoyo's didn't have a chance of beating him. Lew couldn't be sure it had been Roma, of course, but he thought it had. One of Roma's men would hardly burn Santoyo's on his own responsibility. No, it must have been Roma. And before another twenty-four hours had passed, Roma would answer to Lew for this and for every other thing that he had done.

Lew approached the ranch house at .45 carefully, his horse at a silent walk. He dismounted at the corral, tied, then walked across to the lit bunkhouse window. He peered inside, staying back far enough so that his face would not be seen by those inside.

There were four men inside, and this, he judged, was all that was left of .45's big crew. One was the cook. The other three were men who had refused to accompany him when he went after Roma two days before. They'd be no help. The best he could expect from them was neutrality.

He backed carefully away. His shoulder and arm were troubling him now. Exertion had opened the wound, and the bandage was soaked with blood. In addition, loss of blood had weakened him, reduced his stamina. His head felt light; his legs were like lead.

He walked slowly across the open space between the bunkhouse and the courtyard gates. Edging along the wall, he glanced inside, but saw nothing move. Lights were burning in the living room of the house, and in the kitchen. All the separate bedrooms along the walls were dark.

He stepped inside the gates and walked silently through the deep dust of the courtyard toward the big front door. He was halfway across the courtyard when the moon came out from behind the clouds.

The courtyard was suddenly bathed with its cold blue light. And he saw, suddenly, that which he had been unable to see in darkness. There were half a dozen saddled horses tied before the big front door.

Lew sprinted for the protection of the darkened gallery. Behind him, he heard a shout: "Watch the gate! Don't let him get out!"

He didn't recognize the voice. He supposed Roma had laid a trap for him here, a trap permitted by the Regal brothers. They meant that he should die here tonight in the courtyard of .45.

He reached the shade of the gallery and plunged into it. His knees were trembling with the violence of his sudden exertion coupled with the weakness of his wound. He stood in the shadows a moment, listening to the voices echoing back and forth across the yard as they covered the avenues of escape and bottled him up tight.

Under ordinary circumstances, he might still have escaped. As a boy he had often shinnied up one of the gallery poles to the roof, and gone from there over the outside walls. Tonight it was impossible. There wasn't enough strength in his wounded arm to pull himself up. No, if he got out tonight, he would have to fight his way out.

The door of the house opened, and he saw Guy and Ira and a couple of others spill out onto the gallery. They stepped quickly out of the light from the door and lost themselves in the darkness. Lew made a wry grin at their caution.

He considered the situation bleakly. There was a warrant out for him, charging him with murder. Whoever killed him tonight would be in the clear, indeed might even collect a reward for the killing. He heard talking at the far end of the courtyard as they organized their search. He moved quickly along the gallery toward the tied horses, but stopped when he heard a shout:

187

"For God's sake, watch those horses! That's the first place he'll head for."

Almost immediately, he heard the horses pull back on their bridle reins as men moved among them. He hesitated. He drew his gun and held it loosely in his right hand. If they took him tonight, or killed him, it would not be cheap. He would see to that.

And then he heard a voice he hadn't heard before. Joe Riker's voice. "Lew! Can you hear me?"

Lew didn't speak. He waited motionlessly beside one of the stout gallery pillars.

After a moment's hesitation, the sheriff spoke again. "Lew, if you put up a scrap they'll kill you. Most of them are my own posse men from town, but Roma's got two or three men here, too. Give up to me, Lew, and I'll see you stay alive. I'll see you get to town and stay alive until the trial."

Lew couldn't resist a snort of contempt. "Trial for what, Joe? For objecting when Roma tried to take over Forty-Five?"

"He's got a lease, Lew."

Lew snorted again. "What kind of lease? You know as well as I do that lease is no good. Gib had no authority to give a lease."

"It's a matter for the court to decide, Lew."

"And until they do, you'll support it. Is that it, Joe?"

There was a moment's silence. He could imagine the dull red color of Joe Riker's face. Riker knew he was wrong. He was simply yielding to pressure—pressure from Roma, from the Regal brothers, from his own desire to continue on as sheriff.

At last Riker said: "Make up your mind, Lew. You can't get out of here alive."

"You sure, Joe? I know this place pretty well."

A foot scuffed as men moved in toward Lew from the gate. He retreated slowly, stopped when he heard a man's harsh breathing from the other direction. He was boxed on the gallery. Only one path lay open for a retreat, and that was straight out into the courtyard that was lathed with moonlight. Or into one of the bedrooms behind him, where he wouldn't have a chance.

He shrugged resignedly. Perhaps he could have fought his way along the gallery if he'd been willing to kill Riker's posse men from town. But he wasn't.

He called: "All right, Joe! Stop your men and come after me yourself."

All sounds of movement ceased. A deathly silence lay over the place. Tension gripped Lew. This was the test of Riker's courage, of his basic honesty. If he asked Lew to throw down his guns and come out into the courtyard, it would be the same as throwing Lew to Roma's men and Joe knew Lew would have to refuse. But if Riker consented to come after him. . . .

At last Riker said: "All right, Lew. I'm coming." His voice took on an authoritative tone. "The rest of you pull back. 'Way back."

There was some muted grumbling, but it faded as they did as they were told.

Lew was filled with conflicting emotions. One was a deep sense of defeat. Taken by Riker, thrown in jail on a murder charge, he'd be through so far as fighting for .45 was concerned. By the time the trial was held, even if he was acquitted, the fate of .45 would be decided. But the other was relief. J.W.'s worry about him had been unfounded; he was not the way his father had been. He had killed and might again for reason, but he was not a killer, else he would have been unconcerned about the lives of the posse men who were trying to take him. He would never kill wrongfully or from pure uncontrolled rage.

He heard Riker moving along the gallery, walking without stealth. He waited until Riker was abreast, and then said softly: "Right here, Joe."

Riker whirled nervously.

Lew said: "Collect your posse from town and leave Roma's men behind. It's the only way I'll go."

"All right, Lew."

Lew said: "And I keep my guns. I'm taking you on trust, Joe. You'll have to do the same with me."

Riker hesitated over that. But at last he nodded. "Good enough."

He raised his voice and yelled: "I've got him. Smitty, get the horses. You men that are working for Roma get over there by the front door where I can see you."

More minutes of waiting. But at last Roma's three stood grouped before the door, in plain sight.

Riker shouted: "Ira, you and Guy, too!"

The Regal brothers stepped into the light. They made a tight group with the three already there. Looking past them, Lew saw Leona standing in the middle of the living room, clad in a wrapper. Her hair was a mess and even at this distance he could see the pallor of her face. Leona was past the point where she'd fight. She was whipped, beaten. She'd do just as the Regal brothers told her to do.

Discouragement touched him again. He could have beaten the Regal brothers, but the combination of Ira and Guy, Roma and the sheriff had been too much. He swore under his breath. He wasn't through. This was only temporary. He'd go on fighting even if he had to do it from a jail cell.

The posse men led the horses across the moonlit courtyard to where Riker and Lew waited. Riker took a horse and swung up. He said: "Stay on the ground, Lew. Keep the horses between you and that bunch over there by the door. Is your horse out at the corral?"

Lew said: "Yes."

Riker moved out, and Lew walked beside him through the

190

gates. His arm began to ache maddeningly. He wondered where Natalia was, and hoped she was safe. He thought of Slim and Jess, and wondered about them, too. Then they were at the corral, and Lew was untying his horse, the one he'd taken from the man at Santoyo's.

He mounted and they rode out for town, Lew and Riker leading, the others bringing up the rear. As they pulled away, a horseman thundered out of the gate and headed toward Santoyo's.

Lew smiled grimly. He hoped Riker and his posse were prepared to fight for their prisoner. Because when Roma heard what had happened, that was what they would have to do.

XXI

Lew rode in the silent moonlight, Riker ahead of him with one of his posse. The other two rode in the rear. Lew knew if he broke away, or tried to, they'd shoot him down without thinking about it twice. He also knew this posse would never make it to town. One of Roma's men was even now on the way to Santoyo's to get Roma and the rest of his crew, if they could be found. At .45 two of Roma's crew remained along with Ira and Guy Regal. Lew was willing to bet that even now they were saddling up, getting ready to ride. They'd hit the posse first, and hold them in place until Roma could be summoned to take charge. That was why he had insisted on keeping his guns. He might be defeated; he might be killed. But he wasn't going to die without fighting, and he wasn't going to be hanged.

The long, slow miles dropped behind. Lew looked out across the moon-washed land, thinking that he would not see it again for a long time if they ever got him inside that jail. He said abruptly: "Joe, you don't think they're going to let you get to town, do you?"

Riker was silent for a moment. When he spoke, his voice was

an uncertain growl. "They'd better."

"And if they don't?"

Riker swung around. "Damn it, Lew, stop that kind of talk. I'm the law in this county. They wouldn't. . . ."

"Don't count on it," Lew said.

They were now less than five miles from town. Ahead, the road dropped into a dry wash instead of bridging it, and Lew figured, if they were hit at all, it would be here. No other place between here and town afforded enough cover for an ambush.

Lew said—"Joe. . . ."—just as the first shot ripped out ahead. Quartering in, it entered his horse's shoulder, coursed on through to his heart, and came out on the left side, ripping the heel off Lew's boot.

He was out of the saddle before the horse fell, rolling toward the side of the road. One of the posse men behind him, excited and confused, triggered a bullet at him that struck less than a foot from his rolling body.

Riker bellowed—"Dismount!"—but the order was unnecessary, for all the posse men and Riker himself were already on the ground.

Lew lay still, gun in hand, behind a low clump of sagebrush at the edge of the road. The ambushers were hidden in the dry wash ahead, firing from its concealment.

A couple more shots ripped out from that direction, but the flame laced upward from the muzzles and Lew could tell the guns were aimed high over the posse's head.

A voice up there yelled: "We want Lew Stark! Give him up, Sheriff, and we'll save the county the cost of his trial."

Riker's voice was throaty with anger. "Roma? That you?"

"Uhn-uh. He ain't here yet. But he's on his way. He's a man with a bad temper, Sheriff, on account of that foot. If I was you, I'd give Stark up before he gets here."

Riker stood and walked to the middle of the road. He said

harshly: "I've got a bit of advice for you two. Get out of that wash and hit the road, or I'll jug you for attempted murder."

His only answer was a laugh, rudely mocking, and a voice that said: "Sheriff, you've got me half scared to death."

Riker advanced toward them angrily. A rifle boomed and a bullet kicked up dirt in the road two feet in front of his advancing feet. He stopped.

The man said coldly: "Now get on back there and settle down. We'll wait for Roma unless you're of a mind to give us Stark."

Riker turned on his heel and came back to Lew and the others.

Lew waited, giving Riker a chance to think this over. Riker knew as well as Lew did that if he gave up his prisoner, he was through as sheriff. Riker must also know by now that if he did not give Lew up, he was going to have to fight to keep him.

Lew smiled grimly. Riker had his tail in a crack for sure this time.

One of the posse said: "There's only two of them, Joe. Maybe. . . ."

Riker said: "Maybe we could. And then again maybe we couldn't. I don't want any dead men on my conscience if I can help it." He scratched his head, tipping back his hat. He looked at Lew. "What do you think, Lew?"

"You could try pulling back and going around. But it's chancy in this bright moonlight. They're almost sure to hit someone." He gave Riker time to ponder that, and then he said: "Or you could let me go. You and the others could probably make them keep their heads down until I got away."

He felt a certain pity for Riker, but it was tinged with contempt. Riker knew, now, what he had done in agreeing to issue a murder warrant against Lew. He had issued a hunting license, not a murder warrant. The sheriff was probably acutely aware that his agreement to do so had been influenced by other things than simple dedication to duty. This fix he was in was the price of fence-straddling and temporizing. Strict dedication to duty would have spared him all of it.

Riker said: "If I do, will you turn yourself in?"

Lew looked straight at him. "No, I won't. There won't be anything to turn myself in for. Because as soon as you get back to town, you're going to tear up that god-damned warrant. You know who the law-breaker is in this case, Joe, and it isn't me. That lease of Roma's is as phony as five aces in a deck of cards. You know it and you know that Roma's trying to steal Forty-Five. You've got to jump one way or the other, and you're going to have to do it now." He could see the black scowl of anger on Riker's face. He said gently: "Joe, other men have been pressured before you. It doesn't mean you have to go on letting them pressure you. That first bullet was supposed to kill me."

"What would you do if I did let you go?"

"I'd go back to Forty-Five. I'd fight for it if I had to. And I have an idea I will have to."

Still Riker hesitated.

Lew sighed softly. "Joe, I don't expect anything from you. You don't have to take sides until you know which side is going to come out on top. Just let me go. And let me alone."

Even in the pale moonlight, he could see the dark flush that stained Riker's face. Riker wasn't proud of himself right now. He said reluctantly: "All right, Lew. I'll let you go. And I'll tear up the murder warrant. But don't ask for anything else."

"Don't worry, Joe, I won't." He got to his knees and glanced toward the wash. Then he began to ease along the side of the road toward the horses standing, ground-tied, fifty feet away.

From the wash, a rifle boomed, and Lew heard the bullet ricochet on the ground near him and whine away. As Riker and his posse men opened up on the wash, Lew got up and sprinted for the horses.

They spooked away from him, forcing him to slow to an easy walk. Speaking soothing words, he approached and caught one, grinning a little as he recognized the sheriff's mount.

He was under no illusion that he was safe. As soon as the men in the wash heard the drum of hoofs, they'd lose interest completely in the sheriff and his men. They'd be after him. If he managed to get an eighth of a mile lead, he'd be lucky. He swung to the back of the sheriff's horse and spurred away.

Behind, now, the guns of the posse and the answering shots of the men in the wash were like a string of exploding firecrackers. Then, abruptly, all was still.

The road whipped past underneath Lew's horse, which, being the sheriff's, was a good one. But he hadn't gone a mile before he saw, on his left, the dust of a large body of horsemen and a few minutes later saw the horsemen themselves.

They saw him at almost the same instant and changed course sharply to intercept him. Behind Lew, the two that had pursued him from the wash fired their guns in the air and shouted excitedly.

Lew swung right and left the road. This put the galloping bunch behind him. Gradually, as he rode, he began to swing left toward .45.

A surprising thing happened then. The pursuers pulled up in a cloud of dust. After a brief conference, during which the other pair joined them, they split into two groups. One galloped after Lew. The other galloped along the road toward .45.

So that was the way it was going to be. Lew would have bet that Roma was with the bunch headed toward .45. He intended to take it and hold it, leaving Lew no place to go.

Determinedly Lew swung left, taking a course that paralleled Roma's. But the bunch chasing him swung right, forcing him back to avoid collision with them. And they stayed well to the left of him to forestall any future attempts to swing back.

They were almost level with him now, and perhaps a quarter mile away. He frowned worriedly. He *had* to reach .45 before Roma and the others could. He had to get there first and organize some kind of defense.

Recklessly he began to pull left. His pursuers, of which there were three, lined out in single file and began to shoot at him with their rifles. As he drew nearer, their accuracy improved. Lew veered away again. He'd help no one if one of their bullets struck his horse. He'd be afoot; he'd be caught.

He glanced up at the sky. Clouds hung maddeningly close to the moon but showed no indication of drifting across it. His pursuers began to crowd, forcing him even farther to the right.

He galloped on. In the distance now, he could see Roma and the others on the road. Even if he were free right now to head for .45, Roma was bound to reach there first. Roma's three had forced Lew too far off course.

He felt a raging impatience, with his arm, which pained terribly from the horse's movements, with his helplessness. And then he saw something he could scarcely credit. Coming up on his right were two more men.

They were riding hard, bending low over the withers of their horses. When they were within a hundred yards, one of them raised in his stirrups and bellowed: "Lew! Let's take 'em!"

A slow grin touched the corners of Lew's mouth. That was Slim Clark. The chunky, short man with him could be none other than Jess Leonard.

He didn't quite know how they had found him, how they had arrived so opportunely. He supposed they had been on their way to town, or returning from it, and had heard the shots at the wash. Scouting, they had seen Lew ride away, had seen what happened afterward.

They ranged alongside, and immediately Lew swung left,

directly toward the three pursuing him. Slim rode a length behind him, and Jess rode behind Slim. The three raised their rifles and opened up, though the distance was still over two hundred yards.

One of Roma's men shouted with pain as a bullet struck. A moment later, another bullet struck him and he tumbled from his saddle.

The change in odds took the heart out of them. They veered away and back toward town, leaving their wounded comrade behind.

Lew didn't stop. He thundered past the downed man and lined his course straight for .45.

Reaching the road, he turned into it, with Jess and Slim close behind. He could smell the dust raised by Roma's men hanging over the road, and judged they were more than half a mile ahead. Five minutes. That was the time Roma had to secure .45 before Lew could arrive. That was the time spelling out the difference between success and failure for Lew. Roma had five or six men; Lew had two. Ira and Guy and the crew . . . what would they do? What would Leona do? When the chips were down, would Guy and Ira fight for .45 against an invader? Or would it even come to a fight?

Lew didn't know. Right now he didn't care. Anger was building in him until it governed all his thoughts. He'd been hounded, pursued, wounded. He'd been charged with murder and arrested. The ranch had been seized and he had not been able to stop it. He'd seen Santoyo dead, and he'd seen Natalia's home wantonly destroyed. It was time now to fight back; it was time to chase the invaders off .45. It was time to do that or die with the trying. One of old J.W.'s sayings had been that a man filled with righteous anger was the equal of six who carried a sense of guilt. Tonight Lew would put it to the test.

XXII

Roma, riding toward .45, was in the foulest of moods. He was tormented, as was Lew, with pain and the pain was aggravated by the violent movements of his horse. Still, in spite of his irritability, there was a certain savage exultation in him. Lew Stark had been flushed from hiding. And soon he would be killed.

Roma didn't anticipate any trouble in securing .45. He expected no resistance. But he did know he had to arrive at .45 before Lew did or risk a battle for it. Even Ira and Guy Regal might stand with Lew if .45 was directly attacked. The four members of .45's crew might lose their uncertainty under attack. It could turn into quite a job. But not if he beat Lew there.

He put his whole concentration into reaching there first with enough time to spare to secure the place before Lew could arrive. He heard the popping of gunshots behind him on his right, and hoped one of them would cut Lew down. Apparently they did not, for the gunshots continued sporadically until he was almost to the gates of .45.

He reined up just outside the gates, his horse plunging excitedly. He yelled: "Two of you go down to the bunkhouse and get what's left of the crew! The rest of you come with me."

He rode through and stopped again. "French, you and Chavez stay here at the gate. If Lew Stark rides through, cut him down."

He went on across the moon-washed courtyard toward the lights shining from the windows of the house, alone now. He went into the house without knocking, his gun in his hand.

Ira stood up, startled, from one of the sofas. Guy swung from the fireplace, also startled. Before they could speak, Roma said harshly: "I'm taking over here. Lew Stark is on his way."

Ira's eyes showed amazement. "He got away from the sheriff?"

198

Roma didn't bother to answer.

Guy asked: "How many men has he got with him?"

Roma turned to stare at Guy. For the first time it struck him that all this excitement, all this preparation was, so far as he knew, over an impending attack by a single man, and a wounded one at that. He flushed darkly. But, ever honest with himself, he admitted that Lew Stark was the most formidable adversary he had ever faced. A lesser man would have quit long ago. A lesser man would not even consider attacking a ranch turned into a fortress by Roma's men.

Roma also knew Lew wouldn't hesitate an instant. Alone, he'd attack as readily as if he had a dozen men at his back. Roma admitted something else, even more unpalatable than the first admission had been. He was afraid of Lew. So afraid that he would kill Lew at the first opportunity, without mercy and without hesitation. Lew Stark was all that stood between Roma and the realization of a lifelong ambition.

The door slammed open, and the men he had sent to the bunkhouse herded the three members of the crew and the cook inside. All the men were in their long underwear. The cook carried a pair of pants that he now proceeded to don hastily. All wore angry scowls. One was staggering slightly and bleeding from a nasty cut on the forehead.

Roma said: "Herd 'em over in one corner of the room. One of you hold 'em there. The other I want up on the roof of the house. Get going. We've got two men at the gate. Shoot anything else that moves."

The man went outside, and Roma could hear him climbing to the gallery roof and from there to the roof of the house. Roma went outside to the gallery. He moved along it until he stood in the shadow of a supporting pillar, completely hidden in darkness.

So far all was quiet. Roma guessed that not more than three

minutes had elapsed since his arrival. Even the gunshots, the sounds of Roma's men shooting at Lew, had stopped. Roma wondered if they had cut Lew down. If they had, they'd be arriving soon.

A window opened above his head in the second story of the house. He glanced at the gate worriedly, then stepped out from beneath the gallery roof into the moonlight. He looked up.

A woman stood at the window. Leona Regal, he knew. He saw the glint of a gun in her hand, a long-barreled gun that looked like a double-barreled shotgun. She saw him the same instant he saw her, and raised the gun. Roma started to raise his revolver, saw he hadn't time. He dived frantically for the shelter of the gallery.

The shotgun roared, sounding almost like a cannon in the courtyard enclosure. Buckshot raised sprays of dust over a ten-foot circle, the way a handful of sand will raise sprays when thrown upon still water.

Something burned Roma's hip, his shoulder, the calf of his right leg. Knowing he'd never make the shelter of the gallery before the second barrel cut loose on him, he rolled, trying to bring his gun to bear. Up in the window, Leona was screeching angry abuse at him.

Roma snapped a shot at her, and heard her long, wild scream of pain. She disappeared from the window. The shotgun, discharging accidentally inside the house, reverberated like a deeply planted charge of dynamite.

Roma got up. He was shaking, and the fact that he was made him furious. He looked at the gate. His lips moved almost soundlessly. "Damn you! God damn you to hell! I'll kill you if its the last thing I ever do!"

Over his head, in her second-story bedroom, Leona began to cry out hysterically with pain.

★ ★ ★ ★ ★

Lew, galloping hard, with Slim and Jess close at his heels, heard the first roar of the shotgun while he was yet three hundred yards from the gate. The bark of Roma's revolver and the second muted roar of the shotgun followed almost immediately.

He swung hard over and reined up his plunging horse in the shadow of the adobe wall. He dismounted, running.

Now, leading his horse, he approached the gate. Ten feet from it, he stopped, listening intently. Down at the bunkhouse all was quiet. Though lamps still burned there, he knew it was deserted. The shots would at least have brought its occupants, if any, to the door.

Everyone, then, was inside the walls. And Roma had the place secured, or there would have been more shooting. Which meant there would be men beside the gate, waiting to cut Lew down the instant he came riding through.

He looked speculatively at the sheriff's horse. Riker wouldn't like this, and Lew liked it little better, but it had to be done.

Behind him, Slim whispered: "What're you goin' to do? There must be a dozen men in there."

"Maybe they're not all against us."

Slim laughed harshly. "I wouldn't count on that."

"I'm not going to." Lew's anger had not diminished. It burned in his heart like a hot and steady flame. It was monstrous to think that strangers would come riding into .45 and seize it without opposition. He remembered the shotgun blast and thought: *No. Somebody gave them trouble. I wonder who it was.*

Faintly, then, so faintly as to seem almost imagined, he heard a woman's cries of pain. The sounds were weird, floating over the silent walls, and sent small chills coursing along his spine. Rosa? Leona? Or Natalia? Wild anger leaped high from the steady burning flame. He spoke over his shoulder: "I'm going in. Cover me from outside the gate."

201

Slim protested: "Hell, Lew, you can't. . . ."

Lew didn't answer. He mounted the sheriff's horse and spurred savagely. The horse leaped under him.

Lew reined him away from the wall, then whirled and charged straight through the gate. As he passed through, he dismounted with a single easy movement.

Guns flared on both sides of the gate, and bullets cut the air where Lew had been but a fraction of a second before. The horse, riderless, tore into the courtyard, terrified and running free.

A rifle boomed from the roof of the house, another from the gallery before it. The horse pitched and bucked across the yard. Whirling then, he galloped back and on out the gate.

Roma yelled: "Get him! Get him, damn you!" There was a quality to his heavy voice that sounded to Lew like fear.

But he was too busy to think about it. He had hit the man on the left side of the gate, bowling him back against the wall. He scrambled toward the man, and his revolver came down in a clubbing motion. It struck with a sodden sound against the side of the man's head. He had struck the man with his left shoulder and was now blinded with pain. His head reeled and brilliant spots danced before his eyes.

On the other side of the gate, French triggered four fast shots at him, all clean misses. Now French stepped back into the shadow of the wall and hastily shoved fresh ammunition into the loading gate of his revolver.

The rifle on the roof and Roma's gun were bellowing with steady precision, raking the walls beside the gate. A rifle bullet showered French with adobe dust and he yelled: "Hey! Damn it, you're shooting at me!"

The firing continued, for now Slim and Jess were firing from both sides of the gate toward the gun flashes on the roof and below on the gallery before the house.

French, still ramming shells into his gun, broke and ran along the adobe wall, leaving Lew alone with the prone body of Chavez, the tracker.

Lew called softly: "Slim . . . Jess . . . come on in, but do it quick."

Slim ducked around the wall and through the gate. At the same time Jess sprinted across the gateway. He hit the ground in a shallow dive and rolled like a ball.

Instantly the guns across the courtyard opened up. French's revolver flashed from the end of the gallery nearest the gate.

Lew dropped to the ground, and Slim followed suit. Jess clawed toward the shelter of the wall. Adobe dust showered upon them from the wall, loosened by the bullets thudding into it.

There was only a narrow shadow here beside the wall, perhaps two feet wide. Between this shadow and the near end of the gallery was an open space of bright moonlight nearly thirty feet across. One man might get across—with luck. Three would have no chance at all. If they went in a group, one or more was bound to be hit. If they went singly, the first might get across but the others wouldn't have a chance.

Lew said decisively: "Stay here. Cover me. Keep that bunch over there pinned down."

Neither man answered, but both began to place careful shots across the courtyard, aiming at gun flashes and moving instantly each time they shot.

Roma yelled: "He's goin' to try crossing that open stretch! Cut 'im down when he does!"

A feeling of fatalism descended on Lew, but he shook it off. With the slugging of Chavez, he had evened the odds a little, but Roma's men still had an overpowering advantage in that they were shooting from cover while Lew's men were pinned against the wall in the open. The shadow of the wall had noticeably thinned in the time he'd been here. Another ten or fifteen minutes and there'd be no shadow left. Slim and Jess would be revealed plainly by moonlight and shot down mercilessly.

Now the guns across the courtyard were silent. Jess and Slim kept shooting, but they failed to draw return fire. Lew's eyes narrowed. All three opposing guns were trained on the open stretch he had to cross. The instant he moved, they'd belch their flame and death. If he reached the other side, it would be a miracle.

He crouched, gun holstered. Gritting his teeth, he began to run, clinging to the shadow of the wall until he got up speed. Running faster than he had ever run before, he veered away into the pitilessly bright moonlight.

The sound of the guns was a blending roar. A bullet tickled his calf, another slammed against his holstered gun, ricocheted, and whined away into the night. The shock of that sent him spinning, rolling, away from the shelter of the gallery. Behind him Jess and Slim opened up, their guns reloaded now.

Now, however, another sound was added to the uproar. It was that of a shotgun fired from Leona's upstairs window. The buckshot rained across the courtyard, where French now stood. That instant's distraction was all Lew needed. On hands and knees, he lunged for the gallery and made it, rolling the last few feet.

He stood up and fished his gun from the holster. The grips were shattered, a mass of splinters. Probably the action was ruined, too, but there was no place Lew could get another gun. He'd have to take a chance on this one.

Panting heavily, he eased along the gallery, gun in hand. He worked the hammer tentatively and with care. It seemed to be all right. Looking back, he saw Jess's shoulder revealed by moonlight as the man moved. That shadow was disappearing even faster than he had anticipated. He would have to hurry.

He broke into a trot, gun held ready, eyes intent and mouth grim. Across the courtyard, French raked the gallery where Lew was with a probing, aimless fire. One of the bullets shattered a window directly beside him.

Outside the gate, across the plain, Lew heard a distant shout, and could feel in his feet, as well as hear, the drum of many hoofs. Reinforcements for Roma. Defeat. Unless Roma was dead when they arrived.

He called—"Roma!"—and was startled when his eyes caught movement almost directly before him, no more than fifteen feet away. Roma had moved. He'd thought the man was up in front of the house, but Roma had come this way.

Roma's gun flared so close Lew thought he felt the heat of the muzzle blast. A bullet seared his thigh, entered it, and passed on through. Shock almost took his leg out from under him, almost threw him down. By sheer will he flung himself against the adobe wall of the house.

His wounded shoulder struck with all his weight behind it. Pain blinded him and made his head reel. Roma's gun blasted again, but this one missed because of the rapidity with which Lew had moved. Lew raised his gun, knowing he could hit nothing without sighting because of the shattered grips. Probably the sights were out of line as well. Perhaps the gun wouldn't even fire. If it didn't. . . .

Roma made an indistinct, limping shadow as he came toward Lew. His gun roared again, and the bullet splatted against the adobe wall not an inch from Lew's right shoulder.

Lew pointed his gun because he couldn't see the sights. He fired by feel, and fired again. Roma was now no more than eight feet from him. Lew's first two shots appeared to have missed altogether.

He lunged at Roma, jabbed the muzzle of the nearly useless revolver against his chest, and fired. They went down in a fighting tangle, with Roma underneath, and Lew trying to roll away, trying to avoid the muzzle of Roma's gun at this pointblank range.

He became gradually aware that there was no movement in Roma, no life at all. All things seemed hazy and unreal to him. Blood streamed along his thigh and more soaked the bandage on his wounded shoulder.

He got to his feet dazedly. Horsemen streamed through the gate, firing guns, yelling crazily. Their leader was slim and small, and her hair streamed out in the wind.

"Natalia," he croaked, and staggered out into the moonlight.

She dismounted, running. He knew a deep feeling of relief that she was safe, that those moans of pain had not been hers. He realized before she reached him that these horsemen were not Roma's men at all, but Mexicans from the village south of .45. This, then, was where Natalia had gone. She must have ridden like the wind to cover the distance there and back in the time she'd been gone.

She reached him, her face soft, gentle in the moonlight that fell upon it. Her eyes were dark, brimming with tears.

In the courtyard were the sounds of harsh Spanish as the Mexicans rounded up the remainder of Roma's crew.

It was over. It was done. Roma was whipped, but Lew had lost the fight. The Regal brothers and Leona still owned and controlled .45.

Somehow he didn't seem to mind. Something about this girl before him told him that he had gained a treasure infinitely more precious than the one he had lost. Home would be where Natalia was.

She helped him to the door and inside the house. Ira and Guy looked at him sullenly.

Hatred he could have stood. But not sullenness. Fury flared in him, fury that drowned his weakness, that made him forget

206

pain. He looked at them, his face white, his eyes blazing. He said scathingly: "How J.W. could have sired such a pair of sneaking weasels like you two is more than I can understand. You sold out to Roma, but you didn't even have the guts to fight with him."

Neither replied. Neither could meet his eyes. Lew straightened, fighting increasing weakness. He'd not let them see him fall.

Guy mumbled: "Leona is hurt. She wants to see you."

Natalia spoke quickly. "You can't make it up those stairs, Lew."

"Without Leona I'd be dead. I've got to go up."

Natalia did not protest. Instead, she supported him to the stairs and up them. The going was slow and infinitely painful. He reached the top barely conscious. He went into Leona's room with Natalia beside him and collapsed in a chair at her bedside. Natalia rushed to get bandages and began to work on his leg after first gently slitting his trouser leg to make it possible.

Leona lay, pale and weak, upon the bed. She said: "I've been a liar and a cheat, Lew. Forty-Five is yours. J.W. willed it to you before he died."

He looked at her in amazement, his awareness increasing with the shock of her announcement. He said to Natalia: "Never mind me. Look after Leona."

Leona shook her head faintly but determinedly. "Not until I've finished what I've got to say." She put her hand in his. It was cold and clenched, but it held a crumpled scrap of paper. "Call the others," she said weakly. "They've got to witness what I say."

Lew shook his head. "You're too weak. Rest until the doctor comes."

"Call them." There was iron in her now, iron that would not be moved.

Lew nodded at Natalia. She went to the head of the stairs and called down. A moment later, Ira and Guy, with Jess and Slim behind them, came into the room.

Leona said faintly: "This is J.W.'s will. He wrote and signed it in my presence just before he died."

Her hand relaxed; her eyes closed. Lew took the paper from her and passed it to Natalia. She read it aloud.

Ira and Guy filed wordlessly from the room. Slim and Jess glanced at Lew worriedly, then reluctantly followed. Lew looked at Natalia. "How badly is she hurt?" He got up with difficulty and limped to the window.

Behind him he heard bedclothes rustle as Natalia examined Leona. She said: "She's shot in the arm. The bleeding has almost stopped. She'll be all right."

Lew sighed. Natalia came to him and helped him to walk. They left the room together, Lew leaning heavily on her for strength, Natalia seizing eagerly upon the strength he gave to her by his simple need of her.

He would always need her, he thought. He would always want her more desperately than anything else on earth. He had the feeling that somewhere, wherever he was, old J.W. Regal was smiling contentedly at last.

ABOUT THE AUTHOR

Lewis B. Patten wrote more than ninety Western novels in thirty years, and three of them won Spur Awards from the Western Writers of America, and the author received the Golden Saddleman Award. Indeed, this points up the most remarkable aspect of his work: not that there is so much of it, but that so much of it is so fine. Patten was born in Denver, Colorado, and served in the U.S. Navy, 1933-1937. He was educated at the University of Denver during the war years and became an auditor for the Colorado Department of Revenue during the 1940s. It was in this period that he began contributing significantly to Western pulp magazines, fiction that was from the beginning fresh and unique and revealed Patten's lifelong concern with the sociological and psychological affects of group psychology on the frontier. He became a professional writer at the time of his first novel, *Massacre at White River* (1952). The dominant theme in much of his fiction is the notion of justice, and its opposite, injustice. In his first novel it has to do with exploitation of the Ute Indians, but as he matured as a writer he explored this theme with significant and poignant detail in small towns throughout the early West. Crimes, such as rape or lynching, are often at the center of his stories. When the values embodied in these small towns are examined closely, they are found to be wanting. Conformity is always easier than taking a stand. Yet, in Patten's view of the American West, there is usually a man or a woman who refuses to conform. Among his finest titles, always

About the Author

a difficult choice, are surely *Death of a Gunfighter* (1968), *A Death in Indian Wells* (1970), and *The Law at Cottonwood* (1978). No less noteworthy are his previous Five Star Westerns, *Tincup in the Storm Country* (1996), *Trail to Vicksburg* (1997), *Death Rides the Denver Stage* (1999), *The Woman at Ox-Yoke* (2000), and *Ride the Red Trail* (2001), now all available in trade paperback and e-book editions from Amazon Publishing.